Jake looked Savannah over from head to toe, a slow perusal, missing nothing

He noticed the fullness of her bottom lip, slightly moist. Her sweatshirt hugged her body, making it easy to imagine the curves without the clothing in the way. Her fingers were in the front pockets of her jeans, elbows resting lightly against the door. Her back was arched, and he could pretend that was to move her body closer to his. His pulse throbbed with the thought and he took a step toward her, so that a mere foot separated them.

He was drawn to her like a bee to sweet nectar.

"Well?" she said, and he fought to remember what she'd asked him before....

She could easily have pushed him away but she glanced again at his mouth, and in that moment Jake saw the truth in her eyes. She wanted him to kiss her. Savannah still wanted him, whether she would allow herself to or not.

D0837418

Dear Reader,

If you've read either of my earlier Salinger sisters books, you know that the sisters' mom died when they were growing up and that they've all been affected in different ways. (If you haven't read them, you can still enjoy *The Secret She Kept*, since all three books stand alone.) Fear of losing a loved one is something that reaches through all of the Salingers' lives, and Savannah is no exception.

Writing Savannah was a challenge, though. She's controlling and set in her ways. Some (like Jake Barnes) would say she's stubborn. Yet she'd do anything for her children. Maybe even say goodbye to the man she loves...

But first she has to admit she loves him. And before that, she has to admit she doesn't hate him. (See what I mean about being a tough one to write?)

Jake is back in town. And while Savannah's never been easy to get to know, now she's more closemouthed than ever. It's funny, though, how secrets always seem to get out...and turn upside down the lives of everyone involved.

I hope you enjoy Jake and Savannah's story of how one eleven-year-old secret changes their lives for the better... eventually.

I love to hear from readers. E-mail me your thoughts on *The Secret She Kept* at amyknupp@amyknupp.com. Or visit me at one of my online homes: www.amyknupp.com or www.writemindedblog.com.

Thank you for picking up *The Secret She Kept*!

Happy reading,

Amy Knupp

THE SECRET SHE KEPT
Amy Knupp

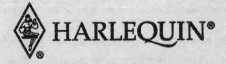

TORONTO • NEW YORK • LONDON
AMSTERDAM • PARIS • SYDNEY • HAMBURG
STOCKHOLM • ATHENS • TOKYO • MILAN • MADRID
PRAGUE • WARSAW • BUDAPEST • AUCKLAND

Recycling programs
for this product may
not exist in your area.

ISBN-13: 978-0-373-71537-4
ISBN-10:   0-373-71537-4

THE SECRET SHE KEPT

www.eHarlequin.com

Printed in U.S.A.

ABOUT THE AUTHOR

Amy Knupp lives in Kansas with her husband, two sons and four cats. She graduated from the University of Kansas with degrees in French and journalism and feels lucky to use very little of either in her writing career. She's a member of Romance Writers of America, as well as the Published Authors Special Interest Chapter (PASIC) of RWA, and shares a blog called Writeminded with four other authors (www.writemindedblog.com). In her spare time she enjoys reading, buying books in excess, traveling, kickboxing, watching college basketball and playing addictive computer games. For more about Amy's books and writing life, visit her Web site at www.amyknupp.com.

Books by Amy Knupp

HARLEQUIN SUPERROMANCE
1342—UNEXPECTED COMPLICATION
1402—THE BOY NEXT DOOR
1463—DOCTOR IN HER HOUSE

Heartfelt thanks go out to:

Sharon Long and Jan Kenny.
Sharon, for redirecting me midstream when I need it
(usually) and Jan, for providing feedback at the eleventh
hour (as well as the eighth, ninth and tenth).
Thank you both for listening, brainstorming,
arguing, laughing and cheering me on.

Roxana Laing, for helping me with art details,
as well as offering ideas for my story.

The Writeminded girls, Jaci Burton, Stephanie Tyler,
Larissa Ione and Maya Banks. You inspire me every
single day with your humor, your work ethic
and your fantastic books.

Kay Stockham and Suzanne Cox,
the very best FNGs ever.
You guys keep me (almost) sane.

Mom and Dad.
Your support means the world to me.

Justin.
Yep, again. I couldn't do what I do if you
didn't do what you do. Thank you.

CHAPTER ONE

SAVANNAH SALINGER DIDN'T like surprises.

Especially when the surprise was Jake Barnes, living, breathing, looking far too good—and standing four feet in front of her. In *her* office. Where she was supposed to be in control.

"Jake," she said, damning the waver in her voice. She stood and walked out from behind her desk toward him. Her heart jackhammered with a suffocating fear she couldn't take time to either rationalize or dismiss. All she knew was she couldn't let him see how his reappearance affected her. Could *not* let him notice her hands were shaking and sweating.

"Savannah." His frown disappeared as he eyed her with blatant approval. "What a surprise." He eased his mouth into the grin she remembered well—sixty percent cocky, forty percent pure sexy. Fortunately, Savannah was one hundred percent immune to male charm—his and everyone else's—these days.

"What in the world are you doing here?" she asked.

"I have a meeting with Zach Rundle," Jake said. "Two o'clock."

"He has…" She stepped over to Zach's desk, which lay

along the back wall, and glanced at the oversize October calendar where he jotted down his appointments. "A two o'clock with the owner of the Levine land."

She peered up at Jake, eager to determine his reaction to being wrong about his meeting. Anxious to get him out of there.

"That'd be me."

She tilted her head in confusion. "I thought the owner was…Odessa Levine."

"I'm here on her behalf. She's my grandmother."

Savannah opened her mouth, then closed it again. "So we're working with you."

"For now."

"You're the one who's going to sell us the land?" She watched his face for a clue to his plans.

"We'll see how it goes," Jake said, shrugging one shoulder and gazing around the room.

Crossing her arms and leaning against the front of her desk, Savannah perused him, refusing to be intimidated by his nonchalance. Or his good looks.

His dark hair was just long enough to be messy on top, in a fresh-out-of-somebody's-bed way that could pique a woman's imagination. Eyes the color of melted chocolate followed her, missing nothing. He was all angles and tautness and confidence.

"Does Zach realize he's meeting with you instead of your grandmother?"

"I do." At that moment Zach, Savannah's boss and brother-in-law, entered the undersized, overfurnished construction office from the back shop area. He wiped off his hands on his jeans, brushed his brown hair off his face and extended a hand to Jake. "Zach Rundle. You must be Jacob Barnes."

"Call me Jake. Pleasure."

"You never mentioned his name," Savannah said stupidly to Zach.

"You two know each other?" he asked.

"We grew up together." Her chin rose a notch as she met Jake's eyes.

"It's been awhile," Jake said in that deep, husky voice of his, returning her stare, their past hanging heavily between them.

"What are you doing back in town?" she inquired, striving for friendliness.

"Family stuff. Researching land options for my grandma, for one thing."

Zach switched into business mode at the reminder, and the two men headed into the adjacent conference room and shut the door. Savannah slumped into her chair, relieved that Zach hadn't invited her to join them, as he often did.

She closed her eyes, wondering what to do about Jake, and about the way her heart was pounding. Keeping him out of her personal life was of the utmost importance. Yet buying that land from Jake's grandmother was vital to Zach and the company, which of course meant it was vital to her. She had to play nice and focus on their business goal until Jake got the heck out of town. And hope like crazy he'd leave none the wiser.

JAKE STRETCHED HIS LEGS out under the conference table as Rundle went to grab a folder he'd left on his desk.

Fancy running into Savannah Salinger here, on his

second day back in Lone Oak. Sure, it was a one-horse town, but he'd barely left his grandmother's house where he was staying since getting in. Hadn't really encountered anyone besides his grandmother and sister. Nevertheless, the odds of meeting up with the one woman who'd always gotten his attention were slim to none. Especially at a construction company.

He let his mind wander to the last day he'd seen her—his final day in Lone Oak. Nearly twelve years ago. He could still recall her eyes lowering with regret. Embarrassment. Loathing, for both herself and him.

Jake straightened in his chair, every muscle in his body tense as he fought to push the memories aside. He needed to be on an even keel for this meeting, not affected by this hardheaded woman from his past.

Rundle walked back into the room, said hardheaded woman following him.

"Savannah's my detail girl," Rundle said. "She keeps track of everything, so I invited her to join us."

Jake nodded, reminding himself this was just like any other meeting he'd had back in Montana. Merely business.

He tried not to focus on how her sweater stretched across her chest as she settled in the chair next to Rundle. When Jake raised his glance to her face, tension buzzed between them.

"Why don't we get down to business, unless you two have some more catching up to do," Rundle proposed.

"We're caught up and then some," Savannah said.

Jake leaned back in his chair and motioned for the other man to go ahead.

"We're very interested in your grandmother's land."

"You and a long list of others," Jake said. "Seems it's in a particularly hot spot."

"It is. It's along the route the new road will take."

"The one that will shorten the commute time to the university."

"Supposed to turn Lone Oak into a bedroom community. God knows this town could use a boost, before it falls off the map."

Jake leaned forward and rested his elbows on the table. "My grandma has lived on that land for ages. Its value is more than monetary to her. She wants to have a say in what it becomes."

"May I inquire why she sent you to meet with us?" Savannah said.

"She's eighty-one years old. Her mind is sharp, but she has trouble getting around."

"So you came back to town to handle this for her?" Rundle queried.

"I came back for other reasons, but she asked me to check into options while I'm here. I build high-end custom log homes in Montana, so I know a bit about property development."

"I'd say you probably do." Rundle sat up straighter.

"I'd like to get an idea of what you intend to do with my grandma's land."

"We plan to build a whole community. Single-family dwellings, apartments, a couple commercial buildings, a community center with a pool, convenience store and gym. Trees and green space."

"Sounds pretty progressive for Lone Oak, Kansas," Jake said. But he was intrigued. He'd expected the status quo.

"Maybe. Or maybe changes would return the town to what it used to be. Make it once again a friendly community where folks could get to know their neighbors, walk to the store for a loaf of bread."

"That sounds promising," Jake murmured. "My grandmother wants something developed that will be important to people."

"What's more important than homes?" Savannah asked, her tone defensive. "A neighborhood where people can put down roots, settle in, stay for years. That's the goal."

Zach glanced sideways at her, as if he wasn't used to her speaking up at meetings.

"You'll be hard-pressed to find a better plan for your grandma's land," she continued. "Unless you consider a sprawling industrial park a decent idea—"

"What Savannah's trying to say," Rundle interjected, "is that we invite you to hear everyone out. Meet with the others who've expressed an interest in the land. We feel confident our vision is the best thing for Lone Oak."

"I've got another meeting this afternoon, as a matter of fact," Jake admitted. "But I can tell you're both very passionate about this scheme."

Savannah always had been passionate, to a fault. They'd argued over many subjects through the years. It was nice to find growing up hadn't mellowed her.

Jake posed several questions. Rundle had answers for everything, albeit vague ones. But Jake couldn't fault him for that. The guy had no reason to trust him yet. Only an idiot would hand over detailed plans at this stage.

Jake studied Rundle, from his plaid flannel shirt over a

white T-shirt to his calm, steady gaze. Rundle was a couple of years older than him—Jake remembered his name, recalled how his brother had been responsible for the accident that killed Savannah's mom. Interesting that Savannah was working for him and seemed to have gotten over the past. He discovered nothing that suggested arrogance or dishonesty in Rundle now, and he appreciated that. His first impression was that he could work with this guy, and first impressions were usually reliable for Jake.

The worst part of Heartland Construction so far was that Savannah came with it. But he wasn't going to let the past or a woman get in the way of what was best for his grandmother whatever that turned out to be.

Having all the information he required for now, Jake stood and exchanged business cards with Rundle.

"Thanks for your time," the man said. "Give me a call if you'd like more information for Mrs. Levine."

"Will do."

The three of them strolled out of the conference room. Jake shook hands with Rundle again and left, thinking about the development they'd discussed. The project was actually something he could get behind. But ultimately, the decision was his grandmother's. He would advise her as much as she wanted, but the land was hers.

"WHAT'D YOU MAKE OF THAT?" Savannah asked once Jake had left.

Zach put his files down and shrugged. "He was impossible to read. Could go either way. Sounds like he knows his stuff, though."

"What if he chooses someone else?" She hated so

much that Jake Barnes was in a position to affect their entire business.

"Then we find another project." He pulled his attention from the papers he'd been shuffling. "You're too worked up about this, Savannah. There's not a lot we can do except present our case the best we can. We just did that."

In other words, they were powerless. Savannah dragged her hands through her long hair with a huff of frustration. "I have to go get the kids," she said as she extracted her purse from her bottom desk drawer. "I'll see you in a while."

As Jake got on his Harley, helmet in his hands, someone exited the front door at Heartland. Savannah. He was parked along the street about two doors down from her, and couldn't help observing as she moved quickly, single-mindedly, ignoring everything around her.

She headed toward the beat-up blue minivan parked in front of him, her wavy, reddish-brown hair flying behind her, and was about to climb in the driver's side when she spotted him. Savannah stopped in her tracks, those brown eyes of hers focused on him.

She tossed her purse into the van, then stared at her feet for a moment, as if gaining control of her temper or else gathering her nerve. She'd never been the type who needed to bolster her courage. Never worried much if she lost her temper, either, now that he thought about it. He watched her curiously from behind his dark glasses.

He noticed her shoulders rise before she turned toward him and approached. That was strange. Atypical for this normally confident, look-out-world-I've-got-something-to-say woman.

She had plenty to be confident about, too. Dressed in slender black pants that showed off her long legs, and a sweater that fell midway down her thighs and was clasped by a single tie across her chest, she somehow managed to appear sexy and professional at once.

It would've been better for him if she'd aged ungracefully. He didn't want to be attracted to her. Instead, she was just as appealing as she had been as a teenager. More so, actually, because now her curves had filled out completely and she had a look that said she'd lived life and had an inner strength to deal with whatever it threw at her. And yet, as she moved toward him, he detected a hint of…uncertainty.

"Hi," she said softly as she drew to a stop right next to him.

"Hey. What's up?"

She chewed the inside of her cheek briefly. "Zach's plan is the best you'll find."

"I have to make sure of that."

"How can you argue about a place where people want to raise their kids?"

"I can argue anything with you."

She scowled at him, then glanced over her shoulder. She took a deep breath and put her hand on his bike. He eyed her, waiting for her to remove it.

"I never pictured you on a motorcycle."

"You pictured me, though, huh?" He shot her a lopsided grin.

That was all it took to get her to drop her hand. "I didn't say that…." She crossed her arms. "Still just as cocky as ever, I see."

"That's the way you always liked me."

"I never liked you."

"That's not exactly how I remember it."

She swallowed and pierced him with those eyes. "Back to the land… Are you going to sell it to us, or are you just going to play games?"

"You really think I'll tell you my plans?"

Fire flashed in her eyes. Here was a much more familiar Savannah than the one he'd seen so far. A thought occurred to him. "Is there something between Rundle and you?"

Savannah laughed for the first time, and he was yanked back to the days they'd run in the same crowd. That laugh had always made him want to hear it over and over.

"Me and Zach?" she said. "Seriously?"

"You can't expect me to believe you don't have a man in your life." Jake didn't allow himself to consider why he wanted to know.

"I don't. And if I did, I can tell you with total certainty it wouldn't be Zach. He's my brother-in-law."

Jake felt the tightness ease out of his neck. "Seems your interests are pretty wrapped up in this company. Your livelihood, your brother-in-law's, your sister's…"

"That's why I'm standing here in the street, talking to you."

"Wouldn't be caught dead with me otherwise, would you?" Anger from the past seeped into his voice.

One of Savannah's knuckles cracked and Jake remembered that had always been the telltale sign she was pissed, liable to tear someone's head off. Getting a reaction from her satisfied some twisted part of him deep inside.

"Hard to be caught dead *or* alive with someone who disappears for almost twelve years."

"If I recall correctly, I disappeared after you told me to get lost."

She hesitated then. "Are you saying you left because of me?"

Jake couldn't help chuckling as he shook his head. "Don't flatter yourself, sweetheart."

He would never admit the impact her blowing him off had had on him. But it had only been one part of what had convinced him to leave.

Savannah frowned, and he could swear her thoughts turned the air blue. But instead of letting loose as she once would have, she spun on her heel and stalked to the driver's side of the van.

Jake watched her retreat, wanting like crazy to hate her. The fact was, though, that after all these years she still got his blood pumping and his brain fantasizing.

CHAPTER TWO

"YOU HAVEN'T BEEN BY the hospital yet, have you?" Jake's sister stood in the middle of their grandmother's spare bedroom with her hands on her slender hips, her shirt riding up just enough to reveal some kind of flashy jewelry in her navel. Jake noticed the tattooed claw of a dragon wrapped around an Asian-looking flower at her hip and would've laughed if he hadn't known she would tear into him for that, too.

"You've got me here for a week," Jake said. As he glanced from Emily to their maternal grandmother, who was perched on the antique armchair in the corner, he felt something inside himself softening. "Ten days, max."

"You've already been here for two full days." Emily continued to stare at him, her green eyes somehow conveying both steel and affection. "Shouldn't need half that long to do what you came to do."

Jake bent down and took an armload of books from one of the shelves, then carried the pile to the side table next to his grandma. Thinning out her bookshelves—stacked three books deep from the bottom—was yet another task Odessa had decided Jake should tackle while in town. "I came back for *you,* Em. Not for him."

"I told you I appreciate that, but a visit's overdue. If you don't do this now, it'll be too late."

The tears in her eyes were like a physical blow. It wasn't often his hard-shelled little sister cried. Her pleas over the phone had been the only thing that convinced him to return to Lone Oak, for the first time since he'd left.

Jake faced his grandma and picked up the top book from the pile. "John Jakes. *Heaven and Hell.* This sounds like something I might be able to relate to."

"It's part of a series," Odessa Levine said, running her hand over her straight, grayish-white hair. "One you'd probably enjoy if you'd sit still long enough to read it."

"I'll save it for my retirement."

"I'll give it to the library," she said, struggling to prevent the corners of her mouth from tipping upward any more at her grandson's hopeless lack of interest in reading.

"He's dying, Jake." Emily broke in. "You have to set aside your testosterone-induced grudge."

"I said I'd see him. Just not today."

Probably not tomorrow, either.

Trying to make peace with his dad after all these years held about as much appeal as reading the entire works of Shakespeare—which he was sure his grandmother had here in her collection somewhere.

His old man had never been reasonable or the least bit concerned about family ties. If he had, maybe he would've apologized before now. But Jake hadn't waited around for any miracles.

"Maybe it'll go better than you expect with your father." Odessa spoke as she sorted her books into two piles, keepers and ones for the library. This had to be done periodically, she'd explained in earnest, to make room for new books. That, or build an addition onto the house.

"Better than I expect would mean we don't kill each other. I'd never dare to hope for an apology."

"He's different now," Emily stated. "These past few weeks he's been...forced to consider something besides work."

"For the first time in his life."

"That's true. I'm not going to make him into something he's not," his sister said. "He's still the workaholic dad who was never there for us. But facing death has made him reflect."

"He's scared," their grandma said. "Fear does something to people. So does waiting to die."

"If he's so different, why aren't you there now?" Jake asked Emily.

"I visited him this morning. I try to go by every day either before or after work."

"So what else do we have to get done while I'm in town?" Jake asked, knowing any more talk of their father's supposed change would just end up in a disagreement. He collected another stack of books and carried them to the table for sorting.

"We need to go through his house and everything in it," Emily said. "He won't be coming home."

"You going to sell the house? Or move in?"

She shook her head. "I have my own place and I'm happy there. I figured we'd sell it."

"That'll be up to you. I don't plan to be in his will. Don't want a damn thing from him."

Instead of disputing Jake's assertion or scolding him, Emily nodded once, her jaw tight. No matter how unconventional in appearance she was, she'd always liked to dream about being part of a conventionally happy family.

Jake had given that up years ago.

Emily pulled her cell phone from the pocket of her black cargo pants and checked the time. "I have to get to the shop for an appointment."

She stuck the tiny phone back in the pocket, bent to plant a quick kiss on their grandmother's forehead, then turned toward Jake, arms open.

"I'm glad you're here," she said as she hugged him. "Even if you're not."

He held on to her, still processing how much she'd changed in the past four years. "It's great to see you, Em. I'm sorry it's been so long."

Which was the truth. He understood now how stupid he'd been to stay away just because of his dad. He'd flown Emily out to visit him a few times, and their grandmother as well, but it was never often enough.

"I'm taking you to Dad tomorrow." She was halfway down the hall when she spoke

"I'll go by myself." When he was darn well ready. "Demanding woman." Only his grandmother could hear the last bit.

"I'm on her side, mister," Odessa said. "If your dad dies and you haven't even tried to make amends, you'll likely regret it one day."

Jake seriously doubted that. But he knew better than to continue this argument. He'd never win.

"Would you like to hear more about the meetings I had today, or do you just want to talk books?" he asked.

"Let's go to the kitchen to discuss the land while I make

dinner. We can finish the books tomorrow so you can haul them to the library."

Jake pulled her walker around in front of her and moved to her side to help her stand.

"Thank you," she said, then made her way out of the room.

When they arrived at the kitchen, Jake got glasses down for iced tea and his grandma removed the lid from the Crock-Pot on the counter. The aroma of home-cooked ribs made Jake weak in the knees.

"Needs another thirty minutes. Sit down. I'll fix the tea," she told him.

He looked at her skeptically.

"Sit," she repeated sternly. "Quit treating me like I'm helpless. I know I've gotten slower, but if I just give up and stop doing everything, you might as well check me into the old folks' home."

Jake grinned and pulled out two of the chairs at the rectangular farmhouse-style table, then settled into one of them.

"So tell me about these meetings. Anyone worth talking any further to?"

"Both of them, frankly."

After adding barbecue sauce to the meat, she made her way to the table, steering her walker with one hand and holding a glass of tea in the other. As she put the glass down, her hand shook.

"Grandma, would you sit down and let me get the other glass?"

She stopped and stared at him, silently, daring him to say another word.

Jake held his hands up in surrender. "No mystery where the stubborn in this family came from."

When she finally returned with the second glass and lowered herself to the chair opposite his at the table, she began peppering him with questions about the development companies he'd met with.

"Sinclair Harris would like to build big beautiful custom homes on large lots," he told her. "With rolling green lawns and long curving driveways. He's got big ideas."

"Does he realize no one in Lone Oak could afford his mansions?"

"He's of a mind that professors from the university would move into them, in addition to some folks here who he claims could manage financing."

"What's so great about that plan?" his grandmother asked. "What am I missing?"

"You said you wanted the area to look nice. This would definitely be impressive."

"Until the houses decayed from no one living in them."

Jake nodded, acknowledging she was more familiar with the community now than he was.

"What about the other company?"

"Zach Rundle proposed building an old-fashioned neighborhood." He explained in more detail what the man had told him. When he finished, his grandmother gazed at him thoughtfully.

"What do you think?" he asked.

"*That* sounds impressive. But I believe I'm in way over my head." She took a sip of tea. "I shouldn't have kept the land so long. Now I'm not sure I can handle this."

"Of course you can, Grandma. I'm here to help you."

"For a little while. What do I do when you're gone?"

"You call me when you need me. But if I remember right,

you're capable of handling just about anything on your own."

"Tell me about the people you met with. Are they decent folks?"

Jake didn't hesitate. "Based on one meeting, I'd say so."

"If this were your land, what would you do?"

He tapped his fingers on the table as he eyed his grandmother. He knew what his instincts were telling him, but sometimes it was necessary to let reason catch up. Jake thought about the men he'd met with today, about their projects. The call was an easy one. "I'd go with Heartland."

She took another sip of tea, then watched the ice bob as she swirled the glass. "Very well. I believe I'd like to meet these people from Heartland. What's next?"

TUTTLE'S DINER WAS still the only burger joint in town after all these years. That point was driven home for Jake as he sat with his grandmother and her book club at a long table on one side and, when the Monday evening dinner crowd thinned out, spotted Savannah in a booth on the other side.

The place hadn't changed at all since he'd been here. Still the same decor, or lack thereof, still the same aromas from the kitchen. Even the specials handwritten on the board next to the cash register were the same, if memory served him correctly. The sameness was comforting in a way Jake had never expected anything in Lone Oak would be.

"Maybe Jacob could provide us some male perspective," one of the women—either Grace or Mary, he thought—said with an eager grin.

"I haven't read the book," he replied for the seventh or

eighth time. Nor had he been paying attention to their discussion. "But the general male perspective is that the woman is usually right, unless it involves tools or cars."

The group of women, ranging in age from their midfifties to his grandmother's eighty-one, chuckled and made sounds of approval.

"If you'll excuse me, ladies, I see an old acquaintance." Jake probably scrambled up too quickly, but he'd been sitting with his grandmother's friends for well over an hour, and while they were all welcoming and tried to include him, he'd had enough discussion of Jane Austen for one day.

He stopped at the counter and requested a refill for his coffee, and as the waitress topped off his cup, he glanced around at the other customers. He spotted a couple of people who seemed vaguely familiar, but no one he could put a name to. He looked over at Savannah again. She didn't appear to have noticed him yet.

Not until he reached her table did it hit him that she was sitting across from two kids.

"TWICE TODAY. Must be my lucky day."

Savannah jumped in her seat at the sound of Jake's voice. She peered up at his hulking form at the head of their table, then at her children, and she had to fight down the urge to escape. Maintaining a calm facade as she forced a smile was all she could do.

"Jake. What are you doing here?"

"Brought my grandmother up for her book club meeting." He gestured to the table of women on the other side of the diner.

"Is that Mrs. Pope over there?" Savannah asked. "She was a teacher at the grade school until she retired last year."

"Grade school, huh?" Jake eyed the kids curiously, then gestured to the booth she was sitting in. "May I? I'm Jane Austen-ed out."

Savannah glanced nervously at Allie, who'd eaten half her meal before pulling out her sketch pad and losing herself in her drawing. Because she couldn't think of an excuse to turn him away, Savannah moved over so he could sit down.

Jake smiled at Logan and Allie, then faced her. "You said there wasn't a man in your life. I guess I didn't know you had a family."

"What with you leaving town for so long, I'm sure there's a lot you don't know." As soon as she said it, she silently scolded herself for getting defensive.

Jake watched her for a second too long, then addressed the children. "My name's Jake." He extended a hand to Logan, who got up on his knees in the booth and shook it for all he was worth. "What's your name?" Jake asked.

"Logan Michael Moser. This is my sister, Allison Elizabeth Moser. Mom's name used to be Savannah Elaine Moser, but her last name changed to Salinger because she got divorced."

Savannah cringed. Why couldn't she have *two* children giving her the silent treatment instead of just one?

Jake glanced at her, a smirk on his face. "Saves me a couple of questions, anyway," he said. "Would that by any chance be Michael Moser?"

"You know it is." She raised her chin, daring him to say anything about her choice in husbands.

Jake focused on Allie, as if finally noticing she hadn't even acknowledged his presence. "Allison Elizabeth. That's a pretty name," he said to her.

Allie continued to ignore him, working away with her pencil on the sketch pad on her lap.

"Allie," Savannah said firmly.

Her daughter glared at her, then uttered a curt "Hi" to Jake.

"She gets involved in her drawings," Savannah said, unsure why she felt it necessary to explain away her daughter's behavior. The truth was this was status quo, and had been for the ten months since the divorce was finalized. In fact, Allie's anger had begun when Savannah and Michael first split up. She apparently blamed Savannah more than Michael, because she treated him with a fraction of the hostility she showed Savannah.

"You like to draw?" Jake asked Allie. "I drew a lot when I was your age."

That piqued Allie's interest. "Did you draw horses?"

At that instant, it all came rushing back to Savannah—how Jake had been into art during grade school, working extra hard on his projects in art class, proudly but quietly accepting the teacher's continuous praise. It was the one area in which Savannah hadn't had a hope of competing with him. Maybe that was why she'd blocked it from her memory until now.

She tuned back in to their conversation, her stomach gurgling with nausea. Jake was listing shows and contests where Allie could enter her drawings.

"I didn't realize you were still active in the art community," Savannah said.

"I'm not. I haven't been for years, but I'm certain those events are still around. Now it's probably easier than ever to hook up with them. Just look online."

"Can we check on the Internet, Mom?" For the first time in weeks Allie was animated. While that brought a small measure of joy to Savannah, she was also ticked off that Jake was the cause of it.

"Of course we can." She strove for offhandedness, as if having a normal conversation with her daughter was…well, normal.

"Can Jake help me?"

Not on your life. "We can handle it ourselves."

"Mom—"

Savannah held up a hand and gave her daughter The Look, the one that stopped whining in its tracks. And now garnered a hateful glare from her once sweet little girl. Savannah sighed inwardly. "Tell you what," she said without thinking. "When we get home, we'll check into signing you up for that art class you've been hounding me about."

"Really?" she asked, eyes bright.

"Really." Savannah forced a grin. No way would she let Jake be the only one to make her child happy.

Allie squealed and bounced in the booth. "Thanks, Mom! Can we go now? I want to get home and fill out the application right away."

"Logan's still eating, honey. We'll leave soon."

Savannah knew already this was the absolute dumbest thing she'd done for some time. She couldn't afford art classes. Was doing well to afford dinner out one night a week. She'd always been prone to doing stupid things when Jake was around. Why did she lose all semblance of sense in his presence? Besides, what did it matter if Allie thought he was nicer? Of course she would. He didn't have to discipline her or tell her no.

"When are you leaving Lone Oak?" she asked him abruptly.

"Another week or so."

"Don't you have to get back to your job?"

"Believe me, I would've been happier not leaving my job at all. But it's good to see my grandma and sister."

"What about the rest of your family? Your dad? Is he still living?"

"For another couple weeks, or so the doctor says."

Savannah looked at Jake sharply to make certain she'd understood right. "He's dying?"

Jake checked to see if the kids were paying attention, but Allie was drawing again and Logan was pushing a French fry around on his plate and making race car noises.

"Cancer. That's the real reason I'm back." His jaw locked tight and he frowned, but she got the sense it wasn't out of sadness.

"I'm sorry," she said, and meant it. She remembered he and his father hadn't been very close, but she didn't wish losing a parent on anyone. She'd been through that when she was fourteen, and understood what hell it could be.

Jake didn't respond and she didn't know what else to say, although his unspoken emotions were pulling at her, making her want to find out more.

"So you build log cabins in Montana."

"Homes. Big custom jobs. I just got the biggest break

of my life, and here I am back in Podunkville to make up with the old man, who couldn't care less about seeing me."

"What kind of break?"

"You familiar with Tony Clayton?"

"Familiar?" He was only one of the biggest names in Hollywood right now. "Just a bit."

"I'm building a house for him."

"Wow. That's great. A big break, like you said."

"If I make him happy, he's got friends. A bunch of overpaid friends who love to buy second and third homes out in the middle of nowhere."

"So you're hoping this will get you all that business."

"That's what I've dreamed of ever since I started. I've worked toward it for years, and now I'm so close I can taste it."

"Your dad's timing isn't the greatest, huh?"

"Nope." Jake frowned again and admitted, "I haven't spoken to him since the day I left town."

The huskiness in his voice made her wonder at all the things he must be going through. She damned herself for caring, but couldn't seem to help it.

Logan shoved his last fry into his mouth and that was all Savannah needed to excuse them. "We have to go."

Jake glanced over at his grandmother. "And I better return to the hen party. Nice to meet you, Logan and Allie." He held his right hand up for a high-five from Logan, and shared a brief smile with Allie before standing.

Savannah watched him walk away, reminding herself distance was exactly what she required. Especially since she apparently couldn't help herself from caring, no matter how dangerous that was.

CHAPTER THREE

SAVANNAH SWORE as she walked down Main Street toward her office. The double mocha latte she'd just bought overflowed the lid of the cup and burned her wrist. She slurped up the spill before it could run down her arm, but didn't take time to reposition her load. She'd taken the kids to the office after school, as she usually did, then left to buy them a snack. Zach was there somewhere—his truck was out front—but he hadn't been in the main office when she and the children had arrived from school ten minutes ago. Judging by the closed conference room door, she'd guessed he was with a potential client.

Logan and Allie were generally well-behaved kids, but too many things could happen in the blink of an eye, especially with a rambunctious eight-year-old boy unsupervised. She never wanted Zach to regret letting her bring the kids to the office after school each day.

The aroma of chocolate chip cookies fresh out of the bakery's oven wafted from the paper bag in her other hand, making her wish she'd grabbed a cookie for herself, too.

Normally, she packed after-school snacks to save money, but this morning she'd had one crisis after another. Allie had experienced one of her preadolescent hormone imbalances, triggered by finding that the one and only shirt she wanted to wear was still in the dirty laundry. Logan's volcano model for school had somehow suffered nearly irreparable damage overnight, which he blamed on Allie, which started the second shouting match before 8:00 a.m. And that was just the beginning of the morning love in the Salinger-Moser family.

Savannah opened the door to Heartland with three fingers of her left hand. Logan was crouched beneath the spare chair along the wall by the copy machine, aiming his gun, made of LEGO blocks, at his sister. The conference room door was now open.

When she glanced at Allie, Savannah stopped dead. Her daughter, sweet, innocent and unsuspecting—okay, sweet was an exaggeration lately—was sprawled on her stomach on the floor between Zach's and Savannah's desks. Talking to *Jake*, who'd pulled out Savannah's chair and was lounging in it, a smile on his face.

Savannah bit back the exclamation of alarm on the tip of her tongue. She wasn't usually one to panic, and showing fear now would only cause suspicion.

Opening the paper bag, she walked toward her son and held out a soft, luscious-looking cookie.

"Come on out, Logan. You can't eat this under the chair."

"Aw, Mom. You blew my cover."

Savannah cracked a smile in spite of her preoccupation and held out the snack, waiting for him to disentangle himself and emerge.

"Thanks," he said as he grabbed it, breaking it into pieces in his haste.

Savannah braced herself and turned toward Allie and

Jake. "What are you doing here?" she inquired, hoping to sound casual and unconcerned.

"I brought my grandmother in to meet with your boss."

"Where *is* Zach?"

"In the back with her. She wanted to see the custom cabinets the guys are finishing up for someone's house. Next thing you know she'll have some in her kitchen. Logan had me at gunpoint and here I am."

Here he was. She nodded in spite of being entirely unhappy about the situation, and set her coffee, now only half-full, on her desk. Could she dare hope that this second meeting meant Odessa was going to sell to Zach? Savannah couldn't bring herself to ask; she'd find out from Zach later. Instead, she gave Jake a scowl that anyone with a clue would know meant *get out of my chair.*

"Allie here tells me she just had a birthday. Eleven years old. Getting close to being a teenager."

Allie smiled at him, that bright, easy, pre-divorce smile. Savannah barely noticed, though, freaking out anew that her daughter was getting so comfortable with Jake. She wasn't typically a chatterbox.

"Could I have my desk back, please?" Savannah wiped every trace of fear off her face and moved in on him, her tone almost amiable.

Jake remained where he was, his long, muscular legs stretched in front of him. He looked Savannah up and down slowly, and apparently finally grasped that she wasn't in the mood to joke around, because he stood and moved out of the way.

She put her purse in her bottom desk drawer and handed the cookie bag to Allie, who set it aside, then intently resumed her latest horse drawing. Jake was heading toward Logan, and Savannah couldn't wait for him to leave, before he lured both her children into liking him.

"Can we talk outside for a second?" she asked him.

He studied her for another moment before nodding. "If my grandma comes in, please tell her I'll be right back," he said to the kids.

Jake followed Savannah out the door. She tried not to feel the heat of him directly behind her, but she couldn't help being hyperaware of his closeness. She'd always had that problem—knowing exactly where he was in the room, what he was doing, who he was talking to, even if she was in the middle of a conversation herself. Always, ever since they were kids.

Once outside, she took several steps down the sidewalk, away from the Heartland office, so the kids wouldn't see them out the window.

The wind had risen that afternoon and the first hint of fall filled the air. She turned to face Jake and the breeze blew her hair into tangles behind her. She made a mental note to drag the kids' jackets out of storage, and hoped they'd still fit.

Jake leaned a shoulder casually against the stone facade of the ancient building. He was close enough that she caught his scent—outdoorsy with a hint of aftershave. It did things to her, jump-started some kind of physical reaction. Their silence grew as she studied the individual fibers of his navy-blue T-shirt. Inching back a step would be wise, but Savannah didn't like the message backing off would send.

JAKE HADN'T BEEN THIS close to Savannah for almost twelve years, yet the reddish brown waves of her hair were still so familiar, the toffee color of her eyes the shade in the recurring dreams he tried to forget about.

"What's up?" he said, annoyed that he could still fall under her spell after how they'd ended things so long ago.

Savannah's eyes shot from his shirt to his face. "My kids have been through hell with this divorce."

"Losing a parent's tough. We both know that first-hand—"

"Right." She cut him off abruptly. How could he forget how she avoided talking about personal subjects? That it was something they had in common didn't matter. "They're still reeling from it. Especially Allie."

"I'm sorry to hear that."

"Stop being so nice to them. Please." Her chest rose as she took a deep breath. "What I mean is, don't go out of your way to get them to like you."

"Who says I have to go out of my way?"

The joke was met with a glare.

He frowned at her. "Let me see if I understand this. Your kids are hurting, so you want me to be mean to them."

"Don't you dare be mean to them. Just…leave them alone."

"I'm not attempting to be their best friend, Savannah. I was just talking to them, treating them like people."

She closed her eyes for a moment. "I know. What I'm trying to say… Allie's responded to you more in the two times she's met you than she has to me in nearly a year. She's hungry for a grown-up she can love and trust, and you seem to fit the bill because you like to draw horses."

"And you're afraid she'll get attached, then I'll leave."

"You're only here for a visit. She *will* be let down. I don't want her to lose anyone else."

"Don't worry. I won't encourage her—"

The door to the office opened and shut, and he pivoted to find Allie walking toward them. Jake automatically smiled at her as she sidled up next to him and handed him a piece of paper—the horse drawing she'd been working on. At the top, she'd written in fancy block letters, "For Jake."

"His name is Frosty," Allie said.

"He's a beauty. You've got some serious talent, Allie." As he gazed down at her, she shyly dropped her gaze to her feet.

Jake noticed the beaded butterfly clasp holding her shiny blond hair in a ponytail, and then his eyes were drawn lower, to her neck, about two inches behind her ear.

He did a double take. Veered away and looked back a third time to be sure.

Holy mother of...

She had a birthmark there. Faint brown, just larger than a quarter, in the shape of an upside-down crescent moon.

Jake knew his eyes were bulging, but he tried to hide his astonishment by avoiding eye contact with the little girl next to him. Coherency escaped him.

He closed his eyes briefly. When he opened them, they automatically sought out the birthmark again, and he broke out into a sweat.

It was the exact same shape, in the exact same place, as his sister's.

CHAPTER FOUR

SAVANNAH'S GAZE WENT from Jake to Allie and back as he leaned against the stone column and covered his eyes with his hands. He was acting weird, as though he was fighting off a sudden migraine or something. Savannah couldn't figure out what she'd missed.

"Jake?"

He didn't appear to hear her.

Allie glanced up at him then, as if finally noticing his strange behavior. "You don't like my picture?"

Savannah glared at him anew, daring him to ignore her daughter's hurt feelings, but he didn't react.

"It's great, Allie," he said after a moment's hesitation. "The best." He held the drawing out in front of him and stared at it, as if just now appreciating all the detail. "I'll hang it on the refrigerator at my grandmother's house."

"Can I visit you sometime so I can see it hanging?"

"I don't think—" Savannah began.

"Hey, Allie, I have to talk to your mom about something really important. Could you go check on your brother?"

Savannah observed him more closely, her heart picking up speed. Something was definitely wrong. She turned to her daughter. "Go. Make certain Logan's not bothering Zach. I'll be there in a couple of minutes."

Allie's eyes sought out Jake's, but he didn't meet her gaze. She pivoted and headed toward the office, shoulders sagging. How had she become so eager for Jake's attention so quickly? She'd have to unlearn that, and fast.

Jake slid down until he was squatting, braced against the column behind him. Savannah was so unaccustomed to him showing any sign of weakness that she wasn't sure how to react.

"Are you...okay?" she asked finally, in a low voice so Allie wouldn't hear.

Her daughter opened the office door, then looked back at them once again before slipping inside, out of earshot.

Jake sprang up angrily and pushed himself away from the column. "When were you going to tell me?" The tightly controlled rage in his voice was unmistakable.

"Tell you what?" But something inside Savannah knew, even before her brain processed the message. She crossed her arms protectively over her chest and sought out the support of the stone wall of the building.

"When were you going to mention that Allie's mine, Savannah?"

Dizziness made her vision blur. She closed her eyes and feared she might throw up as she fought the bile bubbling from deep inside.

"When?" His demand made her jump, and his anger sparked her own.

She uncrossed her arms and straightened, then stepped forward. She shook all over, and clenched her hands to fight the trembling. "I wasn't going to tell you. You were gone."

"It's true then. She's my...daughter." He ran a hand

through his hair, staring into space, unseeing. The tic in his jaw belied the eerie calm that fell over them.

"How did you figure it out?" Savannah asked quietly. "She doesn't resemble you at all—"

"She doesn't resemble me so you planned to take the secret to the grave with you, didn't you? The birthmark on her neck. It's the same as my sister's. Same shape, same place. My dad's mother had it, too. Apparently, it shows up in our family among the females."

Savannah would never have guessed. She'd kissed the mark countless times, but had never reckoned it might make such a difference in their lives. Ever since Jake had returned to town, she'd soothed herself with the reassurance there was no way he could find out the truth....

Savannah slumped against the wall again, in desperate need of its solidity. Her head fell back and hit the stones, but she barely felt it. Her mind became numb. She couldn't form a thought, knew only that her world was falling apart. The security she'd clung to since the divorce was evaporating like a cool mist on a scorching day.

Her chest constricted as she considered Allie. Her baby. Her daughter, who already hated her, yet would need her more than ever if she learned the truth.

Jake had paced down the sidewalk. Savannah took several steps after him.

"You can't tell her. It'll crush her. She's been through so much—"

"Whose fault is that?" He rounded on her, fury in his eyes. "What the hell were you thinking, Savannah?"

She glanced about to make sure no one could hear. "This isn't the place to discuss the subject."

"Forgive me if I'm not too concerned about that."

"Consider Allie, Jake. For one second, think about that little girl and what it will do to her life if she's the talk of the town because of something somebody overheard on the street."

He closed the distance between them, anger radiating from him in waves. He backed her against the wall until their thighs touched.

"You know what I'd like to do right now, Savannah? I'd like to wring your neck!" But he shoved his hands into his pockets. "How could you keep this from me? For all these years?"

In some corner of her mind—a corner she usually kept dark—she'd known this could happen. But she'd never imagined how awful the reality would be.

"I refuse to discuss this with you in the middle of downtown on a public sidewalk," she said. "If you want to talk, we talk later. Tonight. After the kids are in bed. I have to go to them now."

She inched from between him and the wall, but he grabbed her wrist, conveying that he wasn't about to let the matter drop.

"Let me go," she said through gritted teeth.

"Where can I find you tonight? Because we *will* be discussing this in a lot more detail."

"Fifth and Vine. A red duplex. I live in the one on the left. Don't come before nine, because the kids will be awake."

He nodded once but still didn't release her. She pulled on her arm, but he held tight as he stared at her. "I can't believe you didn't tell me."

"Kind of hard to tell you when you *ran away*." She yanked her hand downward and freed herself, then walked toward the office. At the door, she paused and schooled her features to reveal nothing of the tempest inside her.

"Tell my grandmother I went to move her car closer."

Savannah made a point of not glancing at him as she entered.

"Mom! Make Allie stop staring at me like that."

"I'm not staring at him," she said. "Brat."

"Allie. Don't call your brother names. Logan, get your homework out, go to the conference room and start on it."

The little boy groaned, but Savannah barely noticed.

Zach entered from the back room then, helping Mrs. Levine through the doorway with her walker. Thankfully, they'd missed the bickering.

Zach introduced the women and Savannah forced herself to be polite. "It's nice to meet you."

"You, too, dear. Any idea where that grandson of mine is?"

"He went to get the car." Savannah assumed Zach's place to help her to the door.

Mrs. Levine smiled warmly at her. "This young man's got a talented crew. Those custom cabinets are lovely."

"I keep begging them to do some furniture for me, but they claim paying customers come first," Savannah said, vaguely wondering how she was managing to speak coherently, making small talk with Jake's grandma as they headed to the door.

Jake opened it from the outside just as they reached it, and gently took his grandmother's arm. Savannah tried to avoid eye contact and any kind of conversation, but she met his eyes automatically when he touched her arm.

"I'll see you later." His quiet words sounded like a threat.

She let the door swing shut once Jake and Mrs. Levine had cleared it, and went to her desk. There, she sat and shuffled papers to appear busy, even though she couldn't possibly focus on work.

Zach didn't seem to notice anything was wrong. "They're decent," he said. "Had some interesting ideas."

Suddenly, now that she had a crisis to deal with, the land deal wasn't so pressing to Savannah. "What kind of ideas?"

"They proposed forming a partnership just for this project. Mrs. Levine is very interested in what we'd do with the land. She wants to keep her immediate property and the home she lives in, which is close to one edge of the forty acres."

He continued explaining something about varied floor plans and cohesive styles of homes, but Savannah found it difficult to pay attention.

"So where did you end it?" she asked when he stopped talking and waited for her to say something.

"I'm running their partnership idea by my lawyer, first off."

"You're thinking about proceeding?"

Zach strolled around his desk. "I don't think I can pass it up. If this is the only way the project will happen, I can work with a partner. Besides, it'll be cheaper for us in the short term."

"Cheaper's good."

"Tell me what you know about Barnes."

"I thought it was Mrs. Levine's land."

"He'll be in on it, too."

"He doesn't even live here. Why involve him?"

Zach gave her a puzzled look. "Because Odessa Levine wants him involved. She holds all the cards right now. Is there a reason I shouldn't work with him?"

Now Zach seemed suspicious of her, which wasn't at all what Savannah wanted. She struggled to provide him with an honest response.

"Jake is…diligent. Competitive. Loyal until you cross him, then he carries a grudge…."

"Have you crossed him?"

She wouldn't call it that, exactly. "We've known each other since kindergarten. Competed in everything."

"Is that all?"

"What do you mean, is that all?"

Zach studied her, and that made her antsy. She checked her watch, only to find she still had almost an hour to go before she could bow out for the day.

"Maybe what I should ask is whether you can work with him if we make this deal."

"Of course. We need this to happen."

"Last chance. If there's anything I ought to know about Barnes, now's the time to bring it up."

She shook her head. "Go for the deal." Her voice lacked enthusiasm, but it was the best she could do.

Zach stared at her, so she picked up a pen and drew lines under the words on the top paper, as if she was reading intently. Finally, she heard him sit down, reach for the phone and dial.

Savannah propped her elbows on the desk and shielded her eyes with her hands, still acting as though she was hard at work—when in fact tears threatened. She couldn't let them fall.

What was she going to do? What if Jake told Allie the truth? Her throat swelled and seemed to cut off her oxygen. The tears overflowed at last, dropping onto the paper and turning it into a black-and-white smear.

She sucked in air as quietly as possible, fighting to breathe evenly. Perhaps in a few years, when Allie was old enough to understand, she could handle the news. Right now, after the divorce, Savannah had to rebuild Allie's world. She couldn't bear the thought of Allie having another reason to hate her.

She eyed Allie sideways, from under the cover of her hands. The young girl was sprawled on the floor, drawing again, totally unaware. Good. Savannah wanted to keep her in ignorant bliss for as long as possible. Wanted to mend the rift between them and get their relationship back on track before hitting her with another life-altering shock.

Allie was independent, determined to do things her own way. Her butterfly ponytail holder was so little-girl, her concentration on her artwork so grown-up. She was at that awkward stage, no longer a young child but not yet a teenager. Soon she'd be in middle school and face the craziness that was adolescence.

Savannah ached to hold her and tell her everything would be okay, but she knew too well what reaction that would get.

Tears overflowed anew and Savannah plucked a tissue from the box on her desk to sop them up before anyone noticed. Jake had to understand what was best. He might be mad as a bull at her, but he had to step back and acknowledge how much it would hurt Allie to tell her.

Her jaw stiff, Savannah dabbed her eyes with the tissue once more and took a fortifying breath. Her control was back and she wouldn't permit it to slip away again.

CHAPTER FIVE

JAKE ROUNDED THE CORNERS on the gravel roads too fast and nearly planted himself and his bike in a ditch several times, but he didn't slow down.

He'd been riding for hours. If he'd gone in a straight line, he'd be halfway to Montana by now. The freedom the road offered, however, was an illusion, one he fell for less and less the longer he rode.

All of a sudden he was a father. Something told him that even if he'd had years to digest the news, he wouldn't be used to it. *A father.*

His daughter was eleven. Hardly a child anymore. And all he knew about her was that she liked to draw horses and could be moody and withdrawn around her mother. Something inherited from each of her parents, he thought resentfully. He wondered what else she'd gotten from his DNA besides the talent for art and the birthmark.

The sun had set hours ago, darkening the hilly fields so that he could barely make them out in the dim moonlight. He was just outside Lone Oak now, only minutes away from nine o'clock and the chance to confront Savannah and get some answers out of her.

Just the thought of her made his blood boil. Who did

she think she was, to control everyone else's life? Sure, he'd fled Lone Oak, and he'd admit he'd made damn certain no one could track him down. But a lot of years had elapsed between the night he'd taken off and tonight. Plenty of time for her to find him and fess up.

He made his way to Fifth and Vine quickly, his pulse speeding up as he arrived at her house.

The red duplex could use a coat of paint or two. The place was on a hill, and Savannah's side sat atop two single-car garages. Jake pulled his bike up close to one of them and ascended the crumbling concrete steps.

A screen door was all that kept him out. Peering in, he could see a short hall, with heavy wooden doors on either side. He entered and knocked on the door to the left.

It opened almost instantly, but instead of stepping back to let him in, Savannah barreled into the hallway. She led him outside, down the concrete stairs, and seated herself on the second step from the bottom.

"Nice to see you, too," he said to her back.

"Keep your voice down, please. I don't want to wake them up."

He ran a hand through his hair and glanced around the quiet neighborhood before relenting and sitting down next to her.

"Still mad?" she asked.

"What the hell do you think?" he shot back.

A knuckle cracked in the otherwise hushed night. "Try to stop making it all about you for a minute, and listen to me. You cannot tell Allie about this."

"She has every right to know, Savannah."

Her left hand flew to his knee and gripped it. "You can't. She can't handle it."

He shook his head, weary in every cell of his body. "You haven't changed a bit. You're still all about control, aren't you?" He chuckled, a cold, humorless sound emanating from deep in his throat. "I'd think that after being married and having to play nice with others you'd tone it down a little, but you're still every bit as dedicated to being in charge."

"This isn't about me."

"Oh, yes, it is. You're the one who's been manipulating other people's lives in order to hide the big embarrassment of sleeping with me."

Savannah's jaw dropped and she stared at him. "If that's your opinion, then it just goes to show you don't have the first clue about being a parent."

"I haven't had the chance to be a parent. That was taken away from me."

"You took it away from yourself by leaving town."

JAKE BOLTED UP and paced down the driveway. Savannah waited, her tension skyrocketing.

A couple of minutes later, he came back, his arms crossed over his chest. "What I want to understand," he said in an obviously restrained voice, "is why you've kept this a secret from me. Why you thought I didn't deserve to know I have a child."

Savannah really had no desire to get into the subject, had no desire to relive the past or remember that awful period when she'd been so alone and expecting a baby. Had no desire to justify the decisions she'd made, even though she still, today, firmly believed they'd been the right ones.

But she had to. There was no way out of it. Jake would never stop pestering her until she explained, and she yearned for nothing more than for him to leave her and her children in peace.

"You want to know all about it?" she asked.

He raised his brows expectantly.

"Fine." She gazed at her lap for an eternity, struggling to figure out where to start. What to say. Finally she rubbed her hands over her thighs and jumped in at the beginning.

"I was back at college for spring semester, a month or so after we were together. I did a pregnancy test. Four of them, actually, hoping that if I kept trying, one would give me the answer I wanted. But no, they were 100 percent accurate. I freaked."

Jake sat on the step next to her, but maintained his distance. Distance was what she wanted, Savannah reminded herself.

"I came home the following weekend," she told him. "I'd heard you'd gone before I returned to school, but I thought maybe you'd be back. I went to your house and your sister told me you'd left town permanently. She had no idea where you were."

Savannah wasn't about to go into detail about how his absence had sent her into another downward spiral. She'd needed him then, needed someone to face such an insurmountable problem with her. Someone who was as affected by it as she was.

"You'd run away," she said.

"I didn't run away. If you want to get technical, I was sent away."

"What do you mean?"

He was quiet for several moments. "My dad kicked me

out of the house. He was bent out of shape because I was gone all night that time—with you, but he didn't know that. My sister had gotten picked up by the cops. My dad was in Kansas City for a conference and had to leave early to deal with her problems. He was livid I wasn't around to do so."

"You were always handling your sister's problems. Problems your dad should've dealt with."

"That's why I blew up. That particular battle had been brewing for years—ever since my mom died—and we finally let it all out." He swallowed, staring off into the distance. "It was ugly."

"So instead of just getting out of his house, you got out of town."

"Right."

Neither of them said anything for a long while and Savannah found herself waffling between sympathy for Jake and anger that he hadn't been there for her.

At last, he broke the silence. "You can't hold it against me that I wasn't around. I had no idea what you were going through. Maybe if you hadn't told me what a big mistake sleeping together was, if we'd still been together, I wouldn't have left so easily."

"Don't put the blame on me, Jake."

She had wondered frequently, though, how her life would have been different if she hadn't run scared from him. That was what had happened, even though she'd denied it to herself back then. The morning after they'd made love, she'd flipped out. The feelings Jake had evoked in her were way too intense and out of control and she couldn't handle them.

Then *or* now.

"Michael was home from college that weekend, too."

"Moser."

"Yeah."

"Whom you married." He said it as an accusation.

Savannah stood, unable to keep sitting by Jake, zigzagging between past emotions and the spectrum he was putting her through now. Just being around Jake was like trying to sprint through quicksand.

"Michael and I were friends. We'd already dated several times."

"I remember."

"We went out that weekend. I called him because…well, I guess I wanted to talk about it. I hadn't told anyone and I knew I could trust him."

She'd also known he was "safe." He didn't make her do or feel crazy things the way Jake did.

"We had dinner at Tut's and I was rotten company. Afterward, we went on a long drive and I told him everything. He was really understanding. Offered to help."

"So he popped the question."

Savannah glared at Jake. "No, he didn't pop the question. He offered to help me find you."

Jake apparently had nothing to say to that.

"We tracked you to the bus depot in Denver. He and I even drove there the next weekend, hoping to uncover a clue to where you were."

He shook his head. "I didn't want to be found."

"Obviously. Michael and I hunted for you for weeks. We drove all over to small towns, asking people if they'd spotted you. Called hospitals and police stations.

"My dad never suspected what was going on. I missed

a lot of classes, and when spring break rolled around, my pregnancy was starting to show. I hid it for a while, but I knew I had to tell my father. That's when Michael proposed and I quit school."

JAKE CLAMPED HIS JAW SHUT to keep his comment to himself. Michael Moser had been good enough for her, but *he* hadn't. That she'd turned him away after one night burned him to this day. One nearly perfect night that he could still recollect clearly… Her pale silky skin, ghostly white in the moonlight shining in through the window. The long slender body that had sent him into orbit. The waves of reddish brown hair that had covered her delicate shoulders. He hadn't forgotten a single detail.

That night had resulted in a little girl, he reminded himself.

"What's she like?" he asked, emotion softening his voice.

"Who?"

"Allie. Tell me about her."

Savannah studied him in the near darkness and moved closer, then sat down next to him again, lost in thought.

"She's smart. Not just book smart—she grasps things about life. You already saw she's a talented artist. I never realized she got that from you. I'd forgotten."

"What'd she get from you?"

Savannah smiled, but the smile faded into a grimace. "She's as stubborn and independent as anything."

"She got your eyes," Jake said, surprised at the tenderness he felt toward the child he'd only met the other day.

"She got my big feet and my tangle-prone hair. She's a shy child, normally. Total introvert."

"Where did *that* come from?"

"Some recessive gene buried deep inside one of us, I guess."

"I want to get to know her," Jake said without thinking. Once the comment was out, he didn't retract it. He couldn't deny its source was more than mere curiosity about the person who shared half his genetic makeup.

"That's not possible." Savannah's voice lacked all hint of the gentleness it had held when she'd described Allie. Now it was hard. Unrelenting.

But that was too bad, because Jake wasn't about to be denied. He'd missed eleven years with Allie and he refused to miss more.

"It'll have to be possible. She's my daughter, Savannah. You can't prevent me from getting to know her."

She popped up off the step again.

"Tell me how you're going to work that. 'Hey, Allie, this strange man who just showed up in town out of nowhere wants to hang out with you, and I'm okay with it, even though he's a virtual stranger.' She'll think I've lost it."

"So let her think that."

"You don't understand. She is not at her best now. She's hurting and she hates me. I can't do anything to push her further away."

"I thought you said this wasn't about you."

She spun around and faced him. "It's about *her*, Jake," she hissed. "All about Allie. I can't let her find out that the man she's called Dad all these years…isn't. Not right now. Can't you understand how that might shatter her already very fragile world?"

Jake struggled to see things from the point of view of the daughter he barely knew. Wouldn't she want to have the truth? He couldn't quite imagine what discovering something so shocking and fundamental about who you were would be like. Would it hurt her or help her to learn he was her father? The last thing he wanted was to hurt Allie in any way.

"I'll agree to hold off on telling her. For a little while. It'll probably be easier on her if we get to know each other first."

Why he expected that to appease Savannah or make her reasonable, he wasn't sure.

She shook her head vehemently. "We haven't decided you're going to get to know her."

"I'm her father."

"You could pick up and go at any moment. In fact, aren't you leaving soon?"

"I'll be here for a few more days, and then I'll be back several times if things work out with my grandmother's land. But leaving town doesn't mean walking out of Allie's life. There are such things as phone calls and e-mail. She could even fly out and visit."

Fear washed over Savannah's face. "She's not old enough to do that."

He stood and walked up to her. "I'm going to get to know my daughter. We can work together on this, or you can piss me off and push me. Trust me when I say that won't be to your advantage."

"Are you threatening me?" Her teeth were clenched and her eyes held a vicious protectiveness he'd never witnessed.

"Just explaining where I'm coming from."

"Are you telling me you'll take legal action?"

"I didn't say that, did I?"

"Sure sounded like you did."

"I don't want this to be ugly, Savannah. We have a child together, and both of us have some rights in the matter. All three of us. Allie has the right to know who her father is, and I have the right to know her."

"Simple, isn't it?"

"Dammit, Savannah! There's nothing simple about it. I just found out several hours ago that I have an eleven-year-old daughter I never knew about. You tell me what's simple about that."

"Lower your voice," she said coldly. "You may have rights as her father, but the minute you do her harm is the minute you give those up. Having her overhear you would qualify as doing her harm."

Jake pressed his thumb against his lip. The one thing Savannah was correct about was that if Allie overheard them arguing about his being her dad, it would hurt her.

"You're not the only one who's reeling here," Savannah said. "For almost twelve years, I've been in this without you. Now, suddenly, here you are, barging in and inserting yourself into our lives. Wanting to take my daughter to Montana. It doesn't work that way, Jake."

"Does anyone else know about me?"

"No one. No one even knows I was with you."

Didn't that just figure. She was too embarrassed by her terrible lapse in judgment to tell anyone.

"What's your family going to say?" he asked.

"My family isn't going to find out."

He shook his head in disbelief. "You don't get it, do you? The secret is out. You can't go back, Savannah. I'm her father and I'm not going away. The truth is no longer something you can shove under the rug and pretend everything's okay."

"You think that's what I've been doing?" There went the knuckle crack. "You have no concept what it's like to make the decisions I've had to make by myself because you took off. Keep the baby or not. Marry Michael or not. Let my family in on who the real father of my child is or not. Tell Allie or not. Track you down or not. Not a day's gone by that I've pretended everything's okay."

He held up a hand. "Okay, I get it. I'm sorry." He reached out to touch her arm. "Let's take some time so we can both get used to things."

She pulled away from him.

"We'll talk about it again in a couple of days," he stated.

"You don't understand that I don't want to talk about it ever, do you?" she said.

"Oh, I get it just fine. *You* don't understand that now that I know I have a daughter, I can't walk away."

He stared at her for several seconds and then did just that…walked away. But he'd be back.

CHAPTER SIX

JAKE DETESTED HOSPITALS. The smell, the sounds, the harsh lights everywhere. He supposed that was a natural reaction when you'd been through what he and Emily had with their mother.

He stopped at the information desk and asked for Dean Barnes's room number. The volunteer typed in the name, her nails clicking on the keys. "Room 204," she said, and smiled up at him. Jake wasn't able to fake a smile back.

As he made his way to the elevators, he saw the hallway that led to the emergency room. Against his will, he paused, regarded the corridor to the waiting area, and broke out into a cold sweat.

The whole scene came back to him vividly—he and Emily in the uncomfortable, crowded lobby, praying, holding hands... He'd been twelve and Emily six. He remembered fearing the worst and having those fears confirmed when the doctor emerged too soon. Too soon to have rolled their mother to surgery, or to have spent much effort saving her.

Because it'd been too late.

She'd ended her life with a bottle of pills, and no one at the hospital had been able to do anything for her.

Their father had arrived not long afterward. He'd been teaching a class at the university, fifty-five miles away. Jake had tried numerous times to reach him at his office before he'd finally gotten through, and he'd thought then, surely, his dad would step in and make everything a bit more bearable. A little less nightmarish.

But no, he hadn't. He never did. Instead of helping his children through their grief, he'd buried himself even more in his job. Ironic, since Jake maintained that a big part of his mother's problems had stemmed from her husband's workaholism.

Jake shuddered and hurried past the hallway to the elevator.

Once he stood outside of room 204, he leaned against the wall, thinking that maybe sitting in the E.R. waiting room and remembering the hellish past would be preferable to walking through that door and speaking to his father.

He pushed off from the wall and entered, not giving himself a chance to rethink the visit. This was why he'd returned to Lone Oak. He was doing it for Emily and Emily alone.

The sight of the figure in the single bed stopped him in his tracks. Jake turned and checked the number on the door, which he'd left ajar, to verify this was the right room. The man in the bed did not look like his father.

He was sleeping, and the body outlined by the sheets was half the size his dad's had always been—not fat, just wide…sturdy. Tubes snaked from bedside machines and IV drips, and monitors periodically beeped.

When Jake had left town, his dad had had thick, dark

brown hair. Now it was fully gray. His face was thin, bony, almost unrecognizable. His father opened his eyes, and Jake caught a glimpse of the man he remembered. But those hazel eyes were weary. Filled with defeat.

Jake could tell when recognition struck. His father didn't smile, exactly, but something in his face lightened. "Am I imagining things?" he asked in a weak, gravelly voice. "Is it really you, son?"

Jake took one step forward, feeling uncomfortable. "It's me."

Dean Barnes worked one arm from under the blankets and held it out. Jake looked at the bony, pale hand for several seconds, torn. Torn because this man who barely resembled his father was heartbreaking, but had caused so much resentment and anger in the past.

Jake touched his father's hand, then pulled over a chair to sit on, carefully keeping his distance.

"It's nice to see you," Dean said. "Been too long."

Jake worked to keep his comments to himself. While he couldn't get rid of the years-old anger, he did have the sense to go easy on this man. This dying man. Even as Jake stared at his father's emaciated body, he couldn't quite wrap his head around the fact that Dean was losing his battle with the big *C*.

"Emily asked me to return."

"I'm glad."

A nurse arrived then and Jake stood to get out of the way, relieved at the interruption.

"This won't take long," she told him as she rolled in some equipment.

"I'll wait in the hall." He slipped out before anyone

could protest. Exhaling deeply, he leaned against the wall, searching for a happy memory of his father. After his mother died, there had been very few good moments, but before that… There had to be something.

By the time the nurse emerged a few minutes later, he'd dredged up one happy memory. He'd been five or six, and his dad had bought him his first real wooden bat and baseball. They'd played out in the yard for hours. It was one of the only occasions Jake remembered his dad playing with him.

"All done," the nurse said, her voice friendly yet concerned, conveying sympathy for their situation. Sympathy, Jake realized, that was wasted on him.

He was sad, but not because his dad was wasting away. Maybe that would come. Perhaps when his father passed on. Right now his throat tightened at the realization of all they'd missed throughout his life. The family that wasn't…

His thoughts turned to Allie, his little girl, who made him want to smile even now as he thought about the horse drawing she'd given him.

Sadly, he and his dad had shared almost no connection in the nineteen years they had lived under the same roof. Jake had missed the first eleven years of Allie's life, but he had hope for the future. He wanted to make their relationship special, wanted her to have good memories of things they'd done together, moments they'd shared. He wanted to have everything with Allie that he'd missed with his dad.

With Dean it was too late.

Jake straightened and went back into the room, but his father had fallen asleep. Jake watched him for several minutes, again searching for childhood memories of them together, but the truth was his dad had been at work most of Jake's waking hours. He remembered hearing him slip in the back door after Jake had gone to bed. There were occasions when Jake had woken up as his dad told him good-night and pulled up the blankets, but those were fuzzy. Jake wondered now if they'd been real or just what he'd hoped for.

He could feel his pulse pounding in his temples. He had to get out of here. He would have to come back; he couldn't leave things like this. But he couldn't take more tonight, and maybe his dad couldn't either. Dean had acted friendly, but Jake was certain they'd both felt awkward.

He walked out of the room before his father could wake up.

THURSDAY AFTERNOON, Savannah rubbed her aching neck and struggled once again to concentrate on the work in front of her. She hadn't slept much last night, or the nights before—ever since Jake had found out the truth about Allie and decided he wanted to be part of her life.

The kids, for once, were avidly doing their homework, Allie in the conference room and Logan next to Savannah on the floor. She'd promised them that if they could finish their assignments before she was done with work, she would let them each rent a video. She was a firm believer in parenting by bribery at times, and this was one of them. Her headache had persisted for days now, and she acknowledged she'd been rotten company and a grumpy mother. Both kids probably deserved more than a video rental for putting up with her mood, but that was what she could afford today. Maybe Michael could spoil them this weekend.

She frowned. She still wasn't used to losing her kids every other weekend. They were fortunate their dad cared enough to fight for some regular hours with them, she guessed. Sharing was hard to adjust to for everyone, though. All those instances over the years when she'd secretly wished to be alone in the middle of a sibling battle, and now she finally could be. She just had to learn what to do to keep from missing the kids.

The door from the shop area opened and she glanced up, expecting to find Zach, but not Jake right behind him.

"Hey," Zach said, and immediately busied himself with the phone messages that hadn't been urgent enough to forward to his cell phone.

"Afternoon," Jake said, not smiling. He was still upset, obviously. Well, join the club.

Savannah stared at him, unable to think of a thing to say. She couldn't quite act as though everything was fine, not when she was terrified of what his being around would do to her and her kids' lives.

"Is there any coffee?" he asked, and Zach pointed to the conference room, where they kept the coffeepot and cups.

Jake sauntered in that direction and Savannah hastily popped out of her chair to follow him.

She needed to chill. She knew that, but she couldn't seem to do it.

"Coffee?" he inquired smugly.

"No, thank you. Just checking on my daughter." She shot him a glare of warning—possible because Allie didn't even glance her way. "Why are you here, Jake?"

He poured brew into a disposable cup, his back to her. Then he turned, and she couldn't help noticing how appealing he was even after being, she'd guess, on the future job site with Zach—hair tousled, dusty T-shirt stretched across his sculpted chest.

"I'm here for my grandma. Until I leave town, she's put me in charge of her interests."

"I thought you were in the middle of a crucial project back in Montana."

"I am. Now I'm in the middle of two crucial projects, one in Montana and one in Kansas."

"I just find it coincidental that—" Savannah glanced pointedly at the back of Allie's head "—with everything going on, you decide to invade *here*. Now."

"Interesting choice of words." As he spoke, he ambled toward her. "You make it sound like it's all about you." He stopped right in front of her. Far too near. Infringing on her personal space and then some. "It's not."

Savannah glanced toward Allie again, noticing she was drawing instead of studying. Her daughter appeared to be ignoring them, but Savannah had learned that little ears were usually tuned in when you didn't want them to be.

"Allie, why don't you pack up your stuff. We'll be leaving in a few minutes. Did you get your homework done?"

"Yesss," Allie answered impatiently. But she did as Savannah requested, without ignoring her or fighting. She put her pencil into a pink canvas pouch full of art supplies, and zipped it.

"We're renting videos tonight," Allie told Jake.

"Videos? Cool. What are you going to rent?"

"*High School Musical.* It's my very favorite movie."

Who was this child who was volunteering all kinds of information without being prompted?

"That sounds fun," Jake said, brushing a lock of hair behind her ear as she walked past him.

"You could watch with us."

"No, he couldn't." Savannah practically snapped the words. "Go tell Logan to pack his stuff."

Jake started to trail Allie from the room, but Savannah reached out to stop him. He looked down at where she held his arm and she dropped it fast.

"You touched her," she said in a low voice. "You're being affectionate with her. You're trying to get her to like you." Her words were crazy, she acknowledged, but she felt desperate, as if he was stealing her child away.

He stepped closer, so they were inches apart, and spoke softly, gently. "Savannah. You're being ridiculous. Relax."

Being so close, she could sense his heat, the energy that pumped through him, and she wanted to lean closer. Wanted to hang her head and bury it in his chest, because yes, she was overreacting and she knew it. But...

"I can't relax," she said through gritted teeth. "She's my daughter."

Their eyes met, and the fact that Allie was *his* daughter, too, hung between them. Savannah stepped away, annoyed with herself for the momentary urge she'd had to move nearer to him. She pulled him farther into the conference room, out of sight of the others.

"You're using this project to get closer to her, aren't you? That's why you did it."

He eyed her in disbelief. "I didn't even know about her when my grandma decided to meet with Zach. It's been her decision all along. Completely unrelated to what I learned the other night, after our meeting. Do you really think I'd jeopardize my deal in Montana just to mess with you?"

"You said yourself you wanted to be in Allie's life."

"And I'm going to be in her life. I don't have to play games to accomplish that. Not my style, honey."

With that, he left the room, said goodbye to everyone and went out the front door.

Savannah sat on the edge of the table. She was an idiot. She didn't really believe he was using the construction deal to get closer to Allie. She knew how insane that was now that he was gone. But seeing him saunter into the room with her daughter had sent Savannah into a panic. Made her slip into her annoying out-of-control-because-of-Jake mode.

She put her feet on a chair and lay across the table. The fact was more than just Jake's knowing about Allie bothered her. Added to it was a bone-deep fear that her relationship with her daughter would get even worse.

The sound of Logan giggling at something snapped Savannah out of her self-pity fest and made her realize how easily one of the kids could find her here being pathetic and ashamed. She wearily sat up and slid to her feet, wiped the tears away, then busied herself tidying the coffee area. Which really wasn't messy. She just needed a few moments to regain her composure before facing everyone.

So much for not losing control again.

CHAPTER SEVEN

"MICHAEL ISN'T ALLIE'S biological father." Savannah squirmed and closed her eyes for a moment, then got the nerve to face her two sisters, who were seated on the couch next to her. They'd been bugging her the entire car ride to the bridal shop to tell them what was wrong, why she was so uptight. Now they knew.

Katie, the youngest Salinger sister and the bride-to-be, was smiling, clearly not believing what Savannah had said. She pulled her light brown hair up to the back of her head and secured it with a hairband. Lindsey, the oldest, grabbed Savannah's arm, brown eyes wide, her other hand resting protectively over her pregnant belly. Katie noticed, and then she, too, became serious.

"You're not joking, are you?"

"I wouldn't joke about this," Savannah said as she bolted off the couch and paced.

The fitting room was as big as a living room, in order to accomodate three different pedestals surrounded by mirrors, long wedding-dress trains, and the number of people who invariably accompanied a bride to such ordeals. Today there were just the three Salingers. The other bridesmaid, Eve, couldn't make it, and would have to drop by for her final fitting later that week. Claudia, their stepmother, was also absent, on a weekend trip to Vegas with their dad. This was the last fitting before Katie and Noah's wedding, and the sales associate had gone in search of their gowns.

"Whoa," Katie said. "Scandal in the family. Who, pray tell, *is* the father?"

"Katie," Lindsey scolded. But she, too, waited for an answer.

"Probably someone you don't know. His name is Jake Barnes."

"No way! I totally remember him," Lindsey said. "You used to talk about him nonstop."

The saleslady arrived just then, lugging Katie's dress. "Here is the bride's," she said. "Let's start with you and then I'll go get the other girls'."

Katie slipped her jeans and sweater off her perfect size-six body and walked over to where the woman was removing the plastic covering from the gown. "Thanks—" she read the woman's name tag "—Beth. I don't remember Jake." The last was said to Savannah and Lindsey.

"You could stand to eat a sandwich or two," Savannah said at the sight of her sister's thin frame.

"Stop," Katie said. "I'm starving. Now, who's Jake?"

The bridal shop they were in was located in Topeka. The fact that they didn't know anyone in the city was the only reason Savannah dared to continue the conversation.

"He was in my class from kindergarten on. We competed in everything. Something about him has always egged me on. At first the rivalry was natural. Then he started taunting me and encouraging it. I used to hate him," Savannah said.

"I'm not sure *hate's* the right word," Lindsey mused. "I recall how much you talked about him. Usually complaining, yes, but an unnatural amount of it. I used to think you had a crush on him." She took the dress from Beth and began digging through the layers of material to try to slip it over Katie's head.

Savannah made a sound of disgust, a cross between a grunt and a laugh. "He's always made me crazy. He gets my pulse up every time I'm in contact with him, and I don't mean that in a good way. Not always, anyhow."

"He gets under your skin," Lindsey said.

"Yes. Exactly."

"Then how in the world did you end up sleeping together?" Katie asked this from inside the dress, so she didn't immediately catch the glare Savannah shot her.

When Katie's head finally emerged from the white satin, Savannah made a discreet gesture toward the salesclerk, and Katie mouthed, *Sorry.*

Savannah helped Lindsey arrange the skirt of the wedding dress as the woman left the room.

"It's not like we're ever going to see her again after we pick up the dresses, Van. She doesn't care what we're talking about. So, how did this happen?"

"The usual way."

"She means how did you and Jake get together," Lindsey said as she started fastening the million little hooks down the back of Katie's dress.

Savannah stood aside to admire her sister. "You're stunning."

Katie attempted to turn and primp, but the dress didn't seem easy to move in. "Thanks. Now answer the question."

Savannah sat on a stool in the middle of the room and crossed her arms. "We were at a party one night during winter break my freshman year in college. My friends—the ones I'd ridden there with—had an accident when they went out to pick up snacks. I'd stayed at the party but was pretty freaked out when we heard the news. Jake became Super Caring Guy and took me to visit them at the hospital in Layton so I could stop worrying.

"After I'd gotten reports on all of them—they wouldn't let me in to visit Lisa, who was hurt the worst—neither of us was in the mood to return to the party. We didn't want to go home, either."

Savannah stood again, unable to sit still. "This is the embarrassing part. We went to an old barn near his house. The owners only used one part of it, for a couple horses. It was warm and private."

"The proverbial roll in the hay," Katie said from up on her pedestal.

"Hey, watch it. All I have to do is push you and you'll be tangled in satin for a week." Savannah managed a half grin in spite of how uncomfortable she felt baring all.

The fact was she'd needed to confide in her sisters. Needed to talk to someone about the insanity she'd been going through this past week.

"For once, Jake wasn't trying to get to me and I wasn't trying to one-up him. We just…talked. Something clicked. We connected over losing our mothers, and so much more. We spent the whole night there and it was… well, it was the best sex of my life."

Beth reentered the room, carrying two coral dresses. "Usually, it's the bride we overhear saying that," she commented with a grin, and if Savannah had been the blushing type, she would've been beet-red.

She took her gown and laid it over the end of the couch while she undressed. Lindsey was nearby, doing the same.

"Wow!" Katie called, from the perch where she was stuck. "Your bump has become a bulge!" She pointed at Lindsey's belly.

"I want to touch," Savannah declared, shooting back in time to when she'd been pregnant. "May I?"

Lindsey rolled her eyes and nodded. "A girl can't keep anything private anymore, can she?"

"Hey, I just told you the biggest secret of my life. The least you can do is let me feel the baby kick."

"He's apparently napping this morning."

"The seamstress will be in in a few minutes," Beth told them. "I'll help you two get your dresses on. I hope that baby hasn't grown too much." She looked doubtfully at Lindsey's middle.

Once they were all in their gowns and waiting for the seamstress, Beth left the room to help another bridal group.

Lindsey studied herself in one of the mirrors. "I'm never going to forgive you for getting married while I'm pregnant."

"You're gorgeous even with the bulge," Katie said, and faced Savannah. "So you went back to school, found out you were pregnant? Then what?"

"I attempted to find Jake. He'd left Lone Oak right after our night together. I didn't know what else to do. I couldn't handle it by myself. Mom was gone...."

Both her sisters nodded.

"God, I missed her then."

"I can imagine," Katie mumbled, her face drawn. "Did you find Jake?"

Savannah shook her head. "I tried for weeks. Michael and I had gone on a few dates before the Jake night, and he helped me search. I don't know how I would've gotten through everything without him."

"Why didn't you tell *me?*" Lindsey asked. Savannah could hear the subtle hurt in her voice.

"You were at school, sixty miles away."

"You could've called. I would've been there for you."

Savannah studied her. "Are you now?"

Her sister averted her eyes, smoothed coral satin over her belly, chewed her lip. "I don't understand why you didn't tell me. I came home from school often enough. Getting pregnant by the wrong guy—that's huge, Savannah."

"You think I don't know that? It wasn't something I was proud of, believe me. Once I told Michael, I couldn't figure how anyone else could help me. Only Jake."

Lindsey hesitated, as if imagining what Savannah had gone through back then. "So Michael knew from the beginning you were pregnant with Jake's kid?" she queried. "There was no chance Allie was Michael's?"

"Michael and I never slept together. Not until after Allie was born, actually. When it was obvious we weren't going to find Jake, and I started to show, he told me he was in love with me and offered to marry me and raise Allie as his own."

"Wow," Katie said. "I had no idea."

"No one did," Savannah said. "No one could."

"So does Jake know he's Allie's father?"

"He does now. I confirmed it after he met Allie at my office."

"Oh, my God! That's the guy in the new development, isn't it? Jake. And Odessa Levine." Lindsey said. "I hadn't put the name together with *your* Jake."

"He's not my Jake."

Lindsey closed her eyes for a moment. "Zach doesn't know. You haven't told him, right?"

"I haven't told him, but he knows something's weird between Jake and me. I don't exactly act normal when Jake's around," Savannah said.

"That's wild." Katie shook her head.

The seamstress knocked and entered. "Sorry to keep you ladies waiting."

"Oh, that's okay. We've managed to entertain ourselves," Katie said with a friendly grin. "Lindsey's going to require another yard of satin, though."

Half an hour later, they were back in their regular clothes and walking out to Savannah's minivan. Their discussion had turned to wedding topics ever since the seamstress interrupted them, but Savannah was still preoccupied.

"There's one more thing," she said when they'd all shut their doors, Lindsey in the passenger seat and Katie behind them in the middle row. "Jake wants to get to know Allie. And he wants to tell her the truth."

Lindsey shook her head, as though Jake's idea wouldn't work at all. "Did you tell him she's still adjusting to your divorce?"

Savannah nodded. "What am I going to do?"

"I'm not sure. I think you have to prevent him from

telling her for a while," Lindsey said. "She's not in the right frame of mind to hear that kind of news."

"How long will he be in town?" Katie inquired.

"Another few days. And then he'll be back on and off, he said. Enough to turn our lives upside down."

"You have to give him full access to Allie, as long as he promises not to tell her until you agree." Katie was leaning forward between the two front seats.

"Are you crazy?" Savannah said. "Allie's already met him and considers him the coolest thing since Hannah Montana."

"That's okay," Katie replied. "Let him do things with her if he wants. You can't afford to let this get ugly."

"Did he mention legal action?" Lindsey asked.

"Not really. He did make it clear he'll go as far as he has to."

"I feel being flexible with him is the only way. Don't fight him. Give him what he wants as long as he won't tell Allie he's her father. How much will he really take you up on it when he's hardly going to be in town?"

"She has a valid point," Lindsey said.

"Jake is stubborn. He'll take me up on it as much as he can."

"So what's so bad about it, as long as Allie doesn't learn who he really is? If she likes him…"

"I know that's gotta be scary to think about," Katie said. "But if you're nice and accommodating, he has no reason to push things."

"I don't want them to be alone together. That would make me insane with worry."

"Then be sure to let him know you'll always be with them."

Savannah stared straight ahead, tapping on the steering wheel. "I don't like being around him."

She felt Lindsey studying her, which had always made her fidget. "How do you feel about Jake?"

"I loathe him."

Lindsey had one eyebrow raised in complete doubt.

"Mostly. He pushes my buttons. Makes me do stupid things, say stupid things. I basically morph into this out-of-control idiot whenever I'm with him."

"You want him," Katie said.

"Shut up."

"There she goes with that protesting-too-much thing," Lindsey told Katie.

"Make fun of me all you like, but it doesn't matter if I want Jake or not. I'm *not* going to have a relationship with him."

"I don't get it. You have a kid with him. You want him. He probably wants you. What's the problem?" Katie asked.

Savannah twisted to face her little sister. "*You're* asking me? Miss I'm-Not-Going-to-Fall-for-Noah?" She turned back around. "The problem is that I have tried marriage. Tried and failed. As my dear ex pointed out ad nauseam, I like control too much to be in a partnership of any kind. He's absolutely correct. So while I might have once been dumb enough to believe I could make a marriage work, I won't be making the same mistake twice."

They were all silent for a few seconds.

"That's really sad, Savannah." Katie sat back and buckled her seat belt.

"You guys don't understand what it's done to us. To the kids *and* me. I won't do anything to put any of us in danger of going through that again."

Lindsey shook her head. "You have to do what you feel is best, but let me just say I believe you're making a mistake. Maybe you're meant to be with Jake."

Savannah scoffed and started the van. "You've never even met him."

"No, but he's working closely with Zach. Besides, it sounds like I might, if he's going to be in Allie's life."

"Sounds like," Savannah said. "I know you guys are right. I'll make an effort to be nice. And accommodating. Even though that goes against every fiber of my being."

CHAPTER EIGHT

JAKE MADE HIS WAY UP the stairs to Savannah's place late Sunday afternoon, knowing full well she didn't want to see him. Several days had passed since he'd learned Allie was his daughter, and he'd been fixated on all the years they'd missed. He shared the blame for that, but only to a certain point. He still thought Savannah had had plenty of opportunity to track him down and tell him he had a daughter. He couldn't deny that continued to tick him off, and probably would for a while.

He knocked on her hallway door, hearing a TV on inside and sensing movement. But no one answered. He knocked again and heard Savannah's voice just before she opened the door.

"You need a peephole," he told her. "What if I happened to be a serial—"

"If I'd had a peephole, I wouldn't have opened up," she said in a low voice so the kids didn't hear.

Logan was watching cartoons in the living room, but Allie was nowhere in sight.

Savannah hesitated, then smiled—a forced one, he would guess—and moved back to allow him to enter. "To what do we owe the pleasure?"

Her hair was piled sloppily on top of her head and she wore an old sweatshirt and sweatpants with a hole in one knee. Her eyes were weary and had shadows under them, as if she hadn't slept for a couple of nights. He stepped past her and looked around. "Hey, Logan."

The boy turned his attention from the TV and smiled when he saw him. "Hey, Jake! How come you're here?"

"Logan, that's not polite," Savannah said to her son. She turned back to Jake. "But I'm dying to know as well...."

Allie emerged from a different room then and her face lit up when she recognized Jake. He couldn't deny the power her smile had over him. His *daughter*. And she seemed to like him.

"Hi," she said somewhat shyly, but she moved closer.

"What are you drawing today?" he asked. "More horses?"

"I'll show you. Wait a minute." She went back to the bedroom.

Savannah appeared nervous, still hanging near the door. "Why'd you stop by, Jake?"

"I thought maybe we could all go somewhere for dinner." He glanced toward the kitchen but didn't smell any food cooking. "Did I catch you in time?"

Allie came out of the bedroom again just as he spoke. She cheered and pulled at her mother's sleeve. "Can we, Mom?"

Savannah eyed her daughter. "I already have meat thawed."

"Please?"

"You can save it for tomorrow. It'll keep," Jake said. He studied Savannah's face and could tell she didn't want to go. But if she said no, she'd be the bad guy, and she knew it. Jake was sure he'd hear about it later, but he didn't care. Getting an earful wouldn't be enough to keep him from spending time with his daughter.

"I'd have to take a shower," Savannah said. "I smell like kitchen cleaner."

"We'll wait."

Allie jumped up and down and said, "Yay!" Then she held out her drawing to Jake. It was of a saddle propped up against a barn wall.

"You drew this yourself?" he asked with a smile, knowing she had.

"I used a picture from a magazine."

"I really like it, Allie."

Savannah leaned in to view the drawing upside down, and Jake was shocked that Allie hadn't shown her yet. He remembered that when he'd been Allie's age, he'd always rushed to show his mom his latest work—until she'd died. Now that he thought about it, that was when he'd stopped drawing altogether.

"It's wonderful, honey," Savannah said, but Allie didn't respond.

Jake spotted the hurt that flickered over Savannah's face. She met his gaze then and he braced himself.

"Why don't you go put this on your bulletin board, Allie." As soon as their daughter skipped off, she moved closer and spoke quietly. "You don't have to manipulate me. I've made up my mind to let you get to know her—as long as I'm around, too."

"I'm glad to hear that. It'll make things a lot…friendlier."

"Right. Just remember that. Stop playing games and we'll all be fine."

Her eyes shone with fear and he understood she wasn't happy about any of this. That suited him, because he wasn't, either. But he'd take what little she was offering. The one thing he knew about Savannah was that giving over any control to him killed her. His point wasn't to control. He just wanted to get acquainted with Allie. Being with her mother wouldn't exactly be a hardship, unless they fought nonstop.

Savannah stared at him a long while, those brown eyes piercing his. "I'll just be a minute."

She retreated into what he assumed was the master bedroom. Her sweats hid nothing of her shape and he couldn't help admiring how nice her curves were. He shook his head, determined not to think of her in the same way he had for years and years. He'd had no chance with her in the past, proved by her almost immediate rejection of him after their one night together, and had even less of one now. The only thing he wanted here, he reminded himself, was to form a relationship with his daughter.

SAVANNAH TOOK the fastest shower of her life, praying that Allie was still hidden away in her room with her sketch pad. Savannah didn't think Jake would reveal anything critical but she still didn't want them together without her there.

She dried her hair, then threw on jeans and a black hoodie. Skipping makeup, she found her tennis shoes and slipped them on. She was *not* going to look good for Jake. The second she was alone with him she was going to wring his neck, as a matter of fact. He'd said he didn't play games, but that was exactly what he'd done by asking them to dinner when Allie could overhear. Didn't matter that Savannah had decided to go along with her sisters' advice. How he'd gone about getting to see Allie was the issue.

Savannah poked her head out of her bedroom to note where everyone was. Both kids lounged on the couch with Jake, watching Batman cartoons, from the sound of it.

"Jake?" She motioned for him to join her.

He followed her into the kitchen, which was walled off from the living room and dining area, so the kids couldn't see or hear them.

"Where are you planning on eating?"

He shrugged. "Tut's would work. There aren't a lot of choices here, right?"

"I don't want to go where people will recognize us. In Lone Oak, less than a dinner together could start rumors flying."

"And wouldn't it be terrible if everyone thought you and I were together?" he said sarcastically.

"No, it would be terrible if anyone ever suspected the real reason you're with us."

"You know what, Savannah?"

He advanced on her until they were inches apart and she was backed against the counter. Which didn't take much in this small space. She could smell him and was annoyed that his scent was so familiar, that it still stirred something deep within her after all these years. Even more annoyed that a part of her had the overpowering desire to have it envelop her.

She shook off the weak moment.

"I didn't do anything wrong here," he said. "I'm the one who was kept in the dark and lied to for eleven years."

"I never lied to you." She stood her ground even though their closeness was making her lose her concentration.

"You never told me the truth."

"I've told you why."

"Somehow it's not making me feel any better."

"So now it's all about you, huh?"

He stared at her for a moment and then his lips twitched with the hint of a grin. "I'd almost forgotten what a world-class arguer you are and how much fun arguing with you can be."

"This is fun?"

"Beats sitting around at book club with a bunch of old women." Then he did smile, and it made Savannah's heart catch. She hadn't seen that genuine Jake smile, the not-trying-to-charm-the-ladies one, since he'd been back. Which was a good thing, because the sparks it sent through her were powerful and dangerous.

"We've agreed to dinner, right?" he asked, his eyes penetrating and his body still crowding her, making her want things that she would never take.

"I suppose."

"Let's just go with that. Find out if we can get through it without arguing more. For the kids."

She hesitated briefly, then ducked away from him. "You're treating?"

"I'll treat."

"And we can go where no one will know us?"

She could tell that pained him, but he agreed. She

hollered at the kids to get their shoes and jackets on, and practically rushed from the kitchen to escape the close quarters.

"WHAT'S PERSPECTIVE?" Allie asked Jake after she'd finished her pizza and pulled out her pad of paper.

Savannah shoved her last bite of salad into her mouth. She was ready to be done and out of here. When the hostess had led them to this booth, Jake had insisted on sitting next to her. Instead of acting as though it was a big deal, Savannah had gone along with it, but ever since, they'd been inches away from each other, their thighs sometimes touching.

She wished she could say she wasn't affected by his nearness, the warmth of him along her side, but she'd be lying. She kept inching away surreptitiously, but there wasn't a lot of extra space in the booth.

They'd decided it would be best to get out of Lone Oak if they didn't want to be recognized, and Jake had suggested a pizza place in the nearby university town that his sister swore was the best. So here they were at Luigi's, in Manhattan, Kansas. Savannah had to agree with his sister's assessment. They even had goat cheese for Logan, who was allergic to regular cheese.

Her son frowned at Allie's question. "Can't we go play foosball again, Jake?"

"Logan, we're done with foosball for the night," Savannah said. "Let Jake sit and relax."

"Relaxing is boring."

"Sometimes boring is okay," Jake told him. "I don't think I can handle getting beaten again tonight."

That put a smile on her son's face. She opened her purse

and pulled out the small plastic bag of Lego blocks that she always toted around.

"Smart," Jake said.

"Coping mechanism. Little boys don't do sitting still very well."

Allie pushed her tablet toward Jake expectantly. He turned to a blank page and started sketching something, trying to explain what perspective was. He spoke in terms an eleven-year-old could understand, and Savannah remembered he'd taken care of his little sister after their mom had died. He'd always been pretty close-mouthed about it, but keeping things private in a town the size of Lone Oak was hard.

She had to give him credit for being attentive to *both* her children. He'd played foosball with Logan and paid just as much attention to him as to Allie. That endeared him to Savannah more than she cared to have him endeared.

Between that and the attraction that wouldn't quit, she would have to be doubly on guard whenever they were together.

As Jake finished his sketch, a woman approached their table, someone who'd just come in from the street. She wore black leather pants, a colorful tank top beneath a transparent black shirt, and had multiple earrings and studs in her ears and an emerald stud on the side of her nose.

"Emily," Jake said, standing and putting his arm around her. "You're supposed to be working."

"I'm on break. Called in an order for takeout."

Jake stood back and motioned to Savannah and the kids, introducing them. "This is my little sister."

Oh, yes, his sister. Savannah should have remembered her name. She would never admit to the flutter of jealousy she'd felt before realizing who the woman was. Savannah held out a hand to Emily and greeted her.

"I have to grab my food and get back. No one's there to answer the phone in case it happens to ring for the first time all afternoon." She rolled her eyes. "Stop by the shop when you're done if you want."

"We might do that. See you," Jake said, and sat back down.

"What kind of shop? A toy shop?" Logan asked.

Jake chuckled. "Nothing quite so interesting. Just tattoos."

"Cool!"

"You can have one when you're thirty," Savannah told her son.

"What kind of tattoos does she make?" Allie inquired, suddenly interested.

"Whatever you want," Jake said.

"Same rule of thirty applies to you."

"Do you have any tattoos, Jake?" Allie's eyes skimmed his arms and neck.

"I have one on my back," he told her. "Maybe sometime you can have a peek."

"What's it like?"

"It's a design. Kind of tribal." Jake borrowed her pencil and a napkin and sketched it.

Allie found a blank page in her pad and began drawing something. Logan asked Jake questions about having a sister, apparently thinking having sisters gave them lots in common. While Jake chatted with him and polished off a final piece of pizza, Savannah longed to be back home, safe from the thoughts this man made go through her head.

Several minutes later, Allie held up her notebook. "How do you like it?"

"What is it?" Logan asked.

"A tattoo, dummy."

"It doesn't look like anything," her brother said.

"Tattoos don't have to be objects," Jake told him. "Sometimes a design is so neat it doesn't have to be anything. That's really cool, Allie."

"Thank you," she said, her shyness disappearing.

"I believe you have talent at more than just drawing horses."

"She does," Savannah confirmed. "Horses just happen to be the thing right now."

"At my school art show, I'll have lots of stuff on display. You could come, Jake. It's on Thursday."

"What time does it start?" he asked promptly.

"Six-thirty."

"Sounds like fun. Maybe I'll show up."

Savannah didn't like the idea. Michael was supposed to be at the art fair, and just thinking about how awkward that would be made her squirm. "It'll mostly be just family."

"My teacher said we could invite anybody we want to," Allie announced.

"Jake probably has things to do, honey. It's during dinnertime."

"We'll see," he said in a tone that, to Savannah, held the trace of a threat.

She eyed him sideways, shooting a silent warning his way, but all Jake did was smile smugly and announce it was time to go.

"YOU DIDN'T HAVE TO STAY," Savannah said grudgingly as she walked Jake to the door of her place. He'd waited in the living room while she'd tucked Allie and Logan into bed.

"Oh, I know."

She stepped out into the hallway with him, then shut the door. "So why did you?"

"Thought I'd apologize."

"For?"

They descended the concrete stairs to the driveway in silence. His bike was pulled up along the edge.

"Exposing your children to the world of tattoos," he said with a crooked grin.

"I don't know if I'm more worried about Logan wanting to get them or Allie wanting to design them. I've never seen her so interested in something," Savannah leaned against the garage door with a wry smile.

"How many designs did she do on the way home? Four? Five? And they were decent."

"Don't tell her that." She pushed a strand of her hair behind her ear. "Have you visited your dad yet?"

Jake perused her from head to toe, missing nothing. He noticed the fullness of her bottom lip, slightly moist from her tongue. Her sweatshirt hugged her body, making it easy to imagine the curves without the clothing in the way. Her fingers were in the front pockets of her jeans, her elbows resting against the door. Her back was arched, and he could pretend that was to move her body closer to his. His pulse throbbed with the thought, and he stepped toward her, so only a foot separated them.

He was drawn to her like a bee to sweet nectar.

"Well?" she said, and he fought to remember what she'd just asked him.

"My dad. Yeah. I visited him."

"How'd that go?"

"Wouldn't really call it a rousing success. It was awkward as hell. He was friendly, acted glad to see me."

"But you…weren't."

Jake shrugged. "I've got a lot of years of being pissed at him to get over."

She nodded and glanced at his lips, which was all Jake needed to make him move closer yet.

"Kiss me and my knee will go up faster than you can apologize." She smirked when she said it, her hot breath caressing his face and making him yearn even more to kiss her.

He laughed. "Do you get a lot of dates like that?"

"I don't date."

She could have easily pushed him away, but she glanced again at his mouth, and in that moment, Jake discerned the truth in her eyes. She *wanted* him to kiss her. Savannah still wanted him, whether she would allow herself to admit it or not.

For a minute, he let himself get lost in the desire in her eyes, in the heat that pounded through his veins. Then he forced himself to take an excruciating step back and make her consider what she was missing, even though not tasting those lips or sliding his hands across her skin nearly killed him.

He stared at her for a minute longer, then pivoted and got on his bike. "I'll see you soon. Before I fly out next weekend."

She was flustered. Bothered. Exactly what he'd aimed for. He grinned to himself, put his helmet on and rode off.

SAVANNAH WATCHED Jake ride down the dark street, and didn't move for another five minutes after he was out of sight.

Damn him. He made her body want his, crave him, even though her brain knew much better than to even entertain the idea. She was still shaking from the closeness and that look he'd bestowed on her—one that said he'd like to eat her up inch by aching inch.

The wind was cold now but she stayed where she was, willing it to cool her body and erase the painful tightening deep inside. When her fingers were nearly numb, she finally gave up and went back in, although the empty longing had yet to go away.

CHAPTER NINE

MONDAY AT WORK, Savannah spent too much time reflecting on the night before with Jake. She had a stack of papers to read through, but though she didn't want to think about him, she couldn't seem to get him out of her mind.

She sat at her desk after Zach went home, feeling guilty that she hadn't gotten nearly enough done. She'd promised herself she'd check at least two more items off her to-do list before leaving, and she was at last finished. Just one more task to attend to for Allie. The kids were strangely calm and content—Logan with his Game Boy and Allie with her pencils and sketch pad.

Savannah's obsession with Jake was twofold. There was still the anxiety that lit up like a match to a puddle of gasoline whenever he was with Allie. It was mostly irrational, Savannah realized. She'd figured out he wouldn't reveal their secret without letting her know first. He *would* force the issue someday—and probably soon—but his style wasn't to go behind her back. He'd be up front about it. And Savannah would do everything in her power to convince him to hold off.

Then there was the other half of her obsession—the attraction. The memory of how she'd felt close to him on the driveway last night, and in the booth at the pizza shop. Being near him now brought back how being with him years ago had felt, somehow made the memory fresher and a lot more vivid.

Memories aside, her body still reacted to Jake's, and it ticked her off.

Savannah shook her head and focused on the task at hand. She grabbed a sheaf of card stock and went to the large paper cutter next to the copy machine. Allie had it in her head that she was going to create her own postcards with tattoo-like designs, and she'd asked Savannah to cut some card stock into fourths.

Savannah lined the thin stack of paper along the straight edge of the heavy-duty cutter, trying to ensure the cards would all be the same size. Just as she was about to pull the blade down, the front door opened.

"Hey," Jake said.

Savannah's hand slipped and she caught two of her fingers under the blade. "Ouch!" Pain surged through her, and she saw blood welling before she instinctively grabbed the injured fingers with her other hand. "Don't sneak up on me!" she cried, shaking with fury at her clumsiness.

"I just walked through the door. No sneaking. Came to drop off some papers for Zach." Looking concerned, Jake led her to Zach's empty chair, setting a file folder on his desk as he bent over her. "Let me see."

Vaguely, Savannah thought that if she let go of her injured fingers, they might fall off. She squeezed harder, and tears filled her eyes.

"Allie? Bring some paper towels," Jake hollered. "Quick."

Savannah leaned forward in the chair, feeling light-headed. Her eyes were shut, but she opened one and removed her hand enough to find…blood. Lots of blood.

"Jake." Her voice wobbled. "Can't stand it…"

"It's okay, Savannah. We'll handle it."

She shook her head, which made everything swim. "Not good with blood."

He eased her lower, so her chin was between her knees. "No passing out. It's okay. You're okay."

He gently gripped her injured hand, and Savannah felt more pain as he pressed a towel to it, but she didn't care. She was focused on not falling out of the chair or humiliating herself any more.

"It's all right, Allie." Jake's voice sounded muffled now, but on some level Savannah appreciated that he was making an effort to comfort her daughter. "Is Zach here?" he asked.

"He went home," Savannah said. "We can call him…."

"Shh. Let me check."

She started to sit up, but Jake gently pushed her back down.

"No. Let me." He held her hand tightly and she understood he was surveying the damage. "Oh boy," he muttered in a low voice.

"What?" She shifted again, but he restrained her.

"The bone in your index finger is visible. You'll need stitches."

The spinning increased and she put all her effort into sucking in deep gasps of air and letting them out slowly.

"Get your brother to pack up," Jake told Allie, and Savannah was aware of her going into the conference room and doing as she was told. "We're driving you to the E.R."

"What about Noah?"

"Who's Noah?"

"Doctor. Brother-in-law to be. Dr. Fletcher's office."

"Know the number?"

She didn't, and told him where to find a phone book.

While he was dialing, Savannah lifted her hand toward her face, which was still buried between her legs, and moved the paper towel aside. She wanted to see her injury….

No, she didn't.

"Out of luck," Jake said. "They've gone for the day. E.R. it is."

Allie and Logan were hovering close by now. Savannah could feel their concern. "I'm all right," she told them, trying to sound brave.

"She just needs stitches, guys," Jake said.

"Why is she acting like *that?*" Logan, a veteran of many stitches, inquired.

Savannah didn't hear an answer. Instead, Jake appeared at her side. "Ready to stand?"

She drew in a few more slow breaths and nodded. The key was to not look at her hand. She could do this as long as she didn't glimpse the red stuff.

"Where are you parked?"

"Out front, down the street."

After asking for her purse, which Logan fetched, Savannah directed Jake to lock up for her. All this she did without a glance toward her throbbing fingers.

JAKE THOUGHT NOTHING OF going after the van down the street and picking up Savannah and the kids where she'd stopped and sat on the sidewalk. Caring for Savannah's family came naturally. Which would scare the crap out of him if he stopped to analyze it.

Savannah let him do everything. Drive to Layton to the emergency room, answer the questions and fill out the forms at the check-in, dig through her purse for her insurance card, guide her into the little examining room.

The doctor gave her a painkiller and numbed her fingers, and Jake knew the exact minute the drugs kicked in.

"You can go now. I'm fine," she told him.

He ignored her.

"Mom, it's my first art class tonight," Allie said. "Am I going to miss it?"

"Darn it." Savannah motioned for her purse and pulled out her cell phone. She dialed and waited, but obviously got no answer. "Where *are* those people tonight?"

"Who?" Allie asked.

"Katie. Noah. They've disappeared."

"I'll take Allie to her class," Jake said. "Logan can come with me, and then he and I will drive back to get you. Unless you need us here."

"No. And no."

Jake noticed both kids looking at their mother strangely, curiously.

"Savannah, it's a ten-minute drive back to town."

"We have to pay for class whether I go or not," Allie stated, and he wondered if she was parroting something Savannah had said earlier.

Savannah dialed another number, ignoring all of them. Allie seemed close to tears and Jake reassured her that she'd get to her art class.

Savannah clicked her phone off and swore.

"What's wrong, Mom?" Logan asked.

"Lindsey can't come."

"Kids," Jake said, his frustration mounting, "hang out in the hall for a minute, please. I have to talk to your mother."

Savannah started to object, but he sent her a look that shut her up for once. Logan and Allie went out the door and shut it gently behind them.

"What's that all about?" Jake asked, his patience gone.

"I don't want you to have to chauffeur my kids around...."

"She's mine, too." He drew closer. "I thought we were over this."

"Over what?"

"You not trusting me."

"Of course I don't trust you. You want to rock her whole world by telling her the truth."

"It'll happen soon—make no mistake about it. But I hadn't planned on springing it on her tonight on the way to art class."

Savannah cracked one knuckle on her uninjured hand, but didn't say anything.

"Savannah, this is stupid. You've paid for the class. She wants to go and you can't take her. I'm offering."

She dialed again.

"Who now?" he asked.

"Michael," she said into the phone, and explained where she was and that Allie had a class tonight. She hung up within thirty seconds. "He's on his way."

Jake shook his head and chuckled humorlessly. Once

again, she'd chosen Michael over him. Her ex. She trusted the man she'd divorced more than she trusted him.

He sat back in the horribly uncomfortable chair and stretched his arms behind his head, watching her.

"What are you doing?" she asked.

"Staying with you."

ANY OTHER TIME, Savannah would have protested, but her energy was sapped and her fight just about gone. "It won't be pretty," she warned him—futilely, she knew.

"I'll hold your hand." Jake grinned when he said it, and Savannah embarrassingly thought that might not be so bad. She was such a baby when doctors and needles were concerned. "Where's Michael going to meet the kids?"

"Here. I don't want them waiting in the lobby by themselves."

Jake leaned forward and put his elbows on his knees, appearing ill at ease.

"Are you worried about seeing Michael?" she inquired.

He met her eyes, pausing a moment to absorb what she'd said, then laughed. "No. I'm not worried about Michael. Just don't like hospitals much."

"Who does?" Especially when they were planning to drag a needle in and out of your skin.

"My mom died here. My sister and I waited by ourselves out in the lobby. Talking about whether to let your kids wait out there brought it back."

"Jeez, Jake. I'm sorry." Images of what it must've been like for him and his sister ran through her mind and made her shudder.

She climbed down from the examining table to open

the door and let the kids back in the room. On her way, she stopped next to him and put her uninjured hand on his shoulder.

"Go get your kids," was all he said.

They waited in the way-too-small room until Michael arrived. That took forever, but the doctor still hadn't showed.

Savannah hovered at the door, because she in fact *was* nervous about having Michael and Jake together. If she knew her ex, he'd have an opinion about Jake being with the kids. Specifically Allie.

But she spotted him approaching, and sent the kids to him before he got to the room. They would probably tell him who was with her, but at least there wouldn't be any awkward Lone Oak High reunion moments to suffer through.

Then she turned around and realized she was trapped in that small space with Jake. She gave serious consideration to running after the kids and begging at least Logan to stay.

Her eyes met Jake's and she glanced away. A nervous energy hung in the air between them, and she didn't want to think about what that meant.

"Nice," Jake said.

Savannah climbed back up on the table. "What?"

"The way you orchestrated that so Michael and I didn't come into contact. Which one of us are you protecting?"

"Neither. I'm protecting my own sanity. I don't want you two digging at each other."

Finally, a short, fifty-something doctor strode in and greeted them. "How are you folks this evening?" he asked.

"I'll be better once I'm out of here," Savannah told him. "Not a big fan of needles."

"You won't feel anything but a slight tug."

That didn't ease her fears much.

She must've looked as green as she felt, because Jake stood and walked to her side. "Okay if I hold her other hand, Doc?"

"Of course."

He gently took Savannah's hand in his work-roughened one and ran his thumb over her fingers. She was too nervous about getting stitches to appreciate the tenderness of the gesture, though. She faced away from the doctor and his needle, toward Jake. "You'll never let me live this down, will you?"

"Not a chance, Chicken Little."

She clenched his hand in response to the "slight tug" on her injured fingers, then clamped her eyes shut and broke into a sweat.

By the time the procedure was over, Jake was even closer and her head was resting against his chest. In coping mode now, she breathed in the scent of him, over and over. Listened to his heart beat. Steadily. Quickly?

The thought disappeared when Jake tightened his grip on her good hand. "Savannah. All done."

She sprang upright faster than a teenager caught making out in a car. But Jake didn't release her. She tried to pay attention as the doctor provided care instructions, but caught very little of his advice. The urge to get out of this tiny room before the walls closed in on her was growing....

She shut her eyes again until Jake pulled her off the table to her feet. The doctor was gone.

"You okay?"

She didn't reply, just headed for the door. Once out in

the hallway, she leaned against the wall for a few seconds, willing the dizziness away. Then she finally straightened, starting to feel better.

"You're really a mess, aren't you?" Jake noted, falling into step next to her.

"I'm fine."

"Ma'am! You forgot your papers." A nurse jogged down the hall toward them. "Just sign them and you can go."

Savannah stopped at the nurses' counter, signed, and waited for her copy.

"So fine you forgot to get your discharge papers," Jake said.

"I told you I hate needles—and blood. But I'm much better now." She began walking again. "Isn't this where your father is?"

It was a guess, but his hesitation confirmed she was correct.

They went through the double doors to the lobby and she stopped. "Do you want to visit him before we leave?"

"No." The response was immediate.

"Don't you think you should, while we're here?"

"*Should* should be a dirty word."

"That wouldn't prevent you from using it."

Jake looked down at her, considering. "You want to get home and rest. I can do it another day."

"All right, Chicken Little." She started toward the exit.

"Wait," he said. "Let's go." He indicated the hall that led to the main elevators, and Savannah followed him.

"I'll stay in the hall," she murmured as Jake slowed outside a room on the second floor.

"You wanted me to visit him so bad you can come in

with me and suffer the awkwardness." He was trying for offhandedness, she could tell, but didn't quite pull it off. He suddenly wouldn't meet her eyes, kept glancing at the closed door of room 204.

She figured she owed him one and clasped his elbow. "Party on."

That got half a smile out of him. He opened the door and they went in.

JAKE WISHED HE HAD WARNED Savannah about his father's sickly appearance. Her eyes widened when she saw him, and she gripped Jake's arm.

The old man was sleeping. Because he was facing them, it was easy to tell how hollowed out his cheeks and eyes were.

Savannah regarded Jake and he struggled not to let his reaction show.

"Maybe we should go," he said quietly.

His dad's eyelids lifted and he focused on them groggily. "Jacob? Are you back?"

Jake stepped forward. "It's me."

Dean squinted at Savannah. "That's not Emily."

"It's Savannah. A…friend of mine."

His dad slowly nodded at her. "I'm sorry. They've got me pumped full of morphine. Brain's a little fuzzy. Mind helping me sit up?"

Jake grasped his shoulders and repositioned him, then pushed the button to raise the head of the bed. His dad's arms were alarmingly bony, lacking any muscle.

"Thank you," Dean said once the bed's motor stopped and he was resting at a forty-five-degree angle. "I'm glad you came."

Jake couldn't quite say the same, although maintaining a grudge when his dad was so clearly close to dying was hard. "It's Savannah's fault. She tried to chop off her fingers." He gestured toward her bandaged hand. "Had to bring her in for stitches."

Savannah smiled and waved her injured hand. "Good times," she said.

His dad stared at her for several seconds and then smiled. He gazed at her a little longer, then turned his attention to Jake.

"Jacob, I'd like to talk to you."

Jake tensed. He knew this wasn't going to be about the weather or any cute things he'd said when he was a toddler. He glanced at Savannah, thinking she was probably sorry she'd come. "What's going on?" he asked his dad.

"Well…I'm dying."

His father's humor had never been tongue-in-cheek, so surely he realized he'd stated the obvious. Jake had no idea what to say to that so he just stood there.

"Pull up a chair. You, too, if you want," he said to Savannah, "although this could bore you to tears."

Jake drew over a chair with wooden arms. He offered it to Savannah, who shook her head and mouthed that she was fine. Once Jake sat, though, she lowered herself to one arm of the chair.

They perched there, waiting for his dad to speak. The old man didn't rush. He moistened his lips, and Savannah inquired whether she could get him a drink. He nodded and she walked around to the tall table by the window, to the mustard-colored, plastic pitcher.

After she'd poured him some water and held the cup

for him, he thanked her, and she settled back down on the chair arm.

"I believe I owe you an apology, Jacob. I've not been the best father to you kids."

A rock-hard lump filled Jake's throat.

"I...didn't have the first clue how to be a dad."

"None of us do." It was something he'd thought of constantly since learning about Allie.

"But most men figure it out. Just not me." His dad swallowed, looking pained. He struggled to find the next words. "Work was my refuge. I spent all my waking hours there. Told myself that was what my family needed the most—someone to bring home a paycheck."

An uncomfortable silence stole over the room. Jake decided it best to let the man get it all out.

"Do you guys want me to leave?" Savannah asked.

Strangely, Jake didn't. He would've expected having her here would be the most awkward thing in the world, but the idea of her leaving him alone with his father, with this conversation, made him sweat. He shook his head and touched her arm.

"You're fine," his dad said. "When you get this close to dying, you don't worry so much about the small stuff. Only the big stuff."

Savannah relaxed a couple of degrees.

"I'm sorry I ever told you to leave home," Dean said, his attention fastened back on Jake. "Sorry about so many damn things...." His voice cracked.

Jake leaned forward, resting his elbows on his knees, long-buried sadness making his head feel very heavy. He'd always thought that in the extremely unlikely case his father apologized, he'd feel somewhat righteous, but otherwise unaffected. He'd been wrong.

Savannah put her hand on his back. Her touch seemed the most normal thing in the world in this very abnormal moment.

"The fight that night," his dad began again, "wasn't so much about you staying out all hours. Oh, sure, I was ticked off you weren't there when Emily got in trouble. Mad as hell I had to truck back from the conference in Kansas City to handle things. But you were nineteen. I knew we were lucky you were still hanging around. *I* was lucky you were still taking care of Emily when she was younger. You always did. Always knew what to do for her and for yourself."

He stared out the window toward the lights in the parking lot. When he turned to Jake again, Dean's eyes were moist. "You were more of a father to that girl when you were a teenager than I've ever been."

"I just did what it seemed I needed to do. I didn't know the first thing about it, either." Jake's throat felt thick with myriad emotions—sorrow, regret. Maybe even empathy.

His dad smiled sadly. "You got the dad instinct that I've never had. You'll do just fine when you have kids of your own."

Jake straightened and met Savannah's gaze. They were both thinking that he *did* have a kid. Her eyes widened and she nodded subtly, as if to encourage him to tell his father.

He wasn't ready to do that.

Jake couldn't wait to tell the world that Allie was his daughter, but...not his dad.

He appreciated the old man's apology. It was a start,

never mind that it was darn near too late. Saying he was sorry didn't come easily for Dean Barnes. Yet the father-son closeness that would have been nice his whole life was still missing.

Savannah continued to eye him expectantly, but he directed his attention back to his dad.

"I appreciate the apology. I have to tell you I have a lot of years of anger to get over. Ever since Mom died, at least."

His dad flinched at the words. He gazed at the ceiling for several seconds, then finally nodded, looking defeated. "I imagine you do."

They talked about nothing significant for a few more minutes—mostly Dean and Savannah discussing college football. Jake noticed she was getting antsy, and shot her a questioning look.

"I have to get the kids soon," she said.

He jumped up, relieved at an excuse to depart. Some of his resentment toward his father had lessened with their conversation tonight, but they could only get so far in an hour.

"We have to drive back to Lone Oak," he said.

"You planning to leave town soon?" Dean queried.

"This weekend."

"What day is it?"

"Today's Monday. I fly out on Sunday."

His dad made eye contact then, and Jake could see apprehension in his gaze. Dean wasn't sure he would make it until Sunday.

"I'll be back in Lone Oak the following weekend, though." Again, emotion balled up in Jake's throat, surprising him with its intensity. "I'll try to visit again before I go."

His dad nodded, seeming too fatigued to say another word.

CHAPTER TEN

SAVANNAH AND JAKE DIDN'T speak until they were on the highway from Layton to Lone Oak.

"I don't get it," she finally said. "You can't wait to tell Allie you're her dad, but you wouldn't breathe a word of it to *your* dad."

"It doesn't concern him."

"What do you mean it doesn't concern him? He won't be here much longer, Jake. Allie's his granddaughter. I would've thought that after he apologized to you, you might give something in return."

"You've got the give-and-take element right, but my giving was visiting him in the first place. You don't know our history, so how can you lecture me on what I should and shouldn't tell my dad before he dies?"

"I have an idea of a lot of your history. At least the part from the night we were together."

That one night... So many aspects of their lives had been hugely affected by their decisions and actions of less than twelve hours. She couldn't regret any part of conceiving Allie, but what about Jake's estrangement from his family?

"I'm sorry, Jake. I realize tonight wasn't easy for you."

"Yeah. Can we not talk about this anymore? It'll just piss me off again."

Savannah nodded, ready to be done with this crazy night and the spectrum of feelings it had evoked. The first half of the evening had triggered fear and humiliation, all twisted together. The second… If she'd known walking into Mr. Barnes's hospital room would throw her so deep into the middle of a family war, she would've waited in the car, never mind the hall. The visit had been heart-wrenching, from seeing how frail and weak Jake's dad was, to witnessing Jake's internal battle between anger and forgiveness. She could only imagine the thoughts going through his head, the emotions pulling him in different directions.

She didn't want to be so involved with Jake and his family or their problems. Didn't want to care how any of it affected him. But she couldn't deny that she *was* involved and she *did* care.

NORMALLY SAVANNAH GOT the kids to bed around nine, tidied up the house, then retreated to her bed and a book until she fell asleep around midnight. Tonight was anything but normal, though.

The children were keyed up from the break in their routine, her hand throbbed in spite of the pain meds and her head spun in a non-pain-meds way. She suspected the latter was from being with Jake too much.

She could either lie here and make herself crazy remembering everything, from how she'd embarrassed herself over a few drops of blood to the scene between Jake and his dad, or she could collapse and block it all out.

Denial got her vote.

She'd just turned out the lamp on her nightstand and glanced at the clock—it was 9:37—when her door squeaked open.

"Mom?"

"What's up, Logan?" As tired as she was, the interruption might've bothered her, but tonight she was glad to have another living being in the room with her. Especially one as cuddly as her son.

"I can't sleep."

"Jump in," she said, holding the blankets up for him on the far side of the bed. He crawled to the very center of the mattress, not quite huddled up to her but close enough that she could feel his body heat. "Is something bothering you?"

"Nope."

She believed him. He'd never been the type to hold anything back from her. She listened to the quiet sounds of him—soft breaths and little fidgets—and shut her eyes, savoring the closeness. One day too soon, he'd stop curling up with her, even if he never became as antagonistic as Allie.

"Mom?"

She turned on her side to face him. "Yeah?"

"Why is Jake around us a lot?"

Savannah was momentarily stumped. That was a question she couldn't answer honestly.

"Does he like you or something?"

She hesitated and thought fast. "He likes all of us, honey."

"But I mean *like you* like you. Are you his girlfriend?"

"No."

Logan was quiet while he considered her curt answer. "I think he might," he finally said.

"He's just a friend." She nearly choked then, because *friend* had never been a word she'd use to describe her relationship with Jake.

"But he took care of you when you hurt yourself."

"He was just doing what he had to do, Logan. If Zach had still been in the office, he would've done the same thing."

Logan was quiet again, and she hoped she'd satisfied his questions and that he was drifting off. But no.

"I like Jake." Logan was wide awake and his voice was full of conviction.

"Shh," Savannah said, damning herself for attempting to avoid the topic. "Go to sleep."

She wished she could fall asleep herself, but now *she* was wide awake, and worried about Jake spending too much time with her and the kids. She had to put a stop to that before they asked any more questions.

SAVANNAH SPOTTED HIM the second she got out of the van. Didn't matter that they'd had to park halfway across the school parking lot or that he sat on a shaded bench near the entrance. She'd recognize that relaxed, almost smug pose anywhere. Neither she nor Jake had said a word about the art fair when they'd been together Monday evening, but she wasn't surprised he'd remembered.

"Jake's here!" Allie hollered, and both kids ran toward him.

Savannah swore to herself and glanced around to see if

anyone was paying attention to them. No one appeared to care or even notice, but her heart raced anyway. She knew being so concerned about someone else figuring out Jake's role in their lives was dumb, but her body didn't appear to get the message.

She walked slowly toward them, using every step to reel in her temper. He was going to stick out in the crowd. He didn't belong to anyone else with ties to the school. Savannah would bet he'd get plenty of attention because there weren't many thirty-something men in this town who looked as tempting as he did. He'd have mothers craning their necks wherever he went.

"Can you believe it, Mom? Jake came for our art fair!" Logan high-fived Jake and bounced around as Savannah approached.

"No. I can't." She eyed Jake pointedly, but he just smiled.

"Couldn't pass up such an offer, could I?" He spoke to the kids. "Let's go see your stuff."

They were supposed to meet Lindsey and Zach and their boys, Owen and Billy, to view all four kids' artwork together. Michael was supposed to show up at some point, as well. This had the potential to turn into one giant uncomfortable moment.

"Can we go now, Mom?"

The decision was simple. She nodded. "Let's get started. We'll find Owen and Billy soon. They probably aren't here yet."

Allie and Logan hurried through the double doors to the main hall. Jake put an arm around Savannah to guide her in.

"What do you think you're doing?" She said the words softly enough that no one else could hear.

"You're uncomfortable."

"That surprises you?"

"I figure we can either make it seem that I'm here because I'm interested in you, or because I'm interested in your children."

"Why *are* you here?"

"Why wouldn't I be? Allie invited me." He opened the door for Savannah. "I notice Moser isn't."

"He'll be here sometime." Unfortunately. All she needed was for him to find out Jake was in town, if he didn't already know.

They headed for the second grade halls first, and were treated to a narrated tour by Logan. Savannah hung back with Jake for the very reason he'd mentioned. He'd taken his arm off her, thankfully, because she could have easily gotten used to the way it felt, his fingers caressing her periodically, his heat enveloping her.

She put an extra foot of space between them as she oohed and aahed over Logan's last picture, an acrylic painting of a boat on the ocean. He hadn't been gifted with Allie's talent, but the piece made Savannah smile proudly and hug her boy. Clearly, he'd worked hard on it, from the stripes on the sail to the smiley face on the sun.

They finished praising Logan and moved out of the way of another family. So far so good. They were halfway done, with no sign of her sister's family or Michael yet.

"On to fifth grade," Savannah said, and assumed the lead at a quick pace.

At the beginning of the fifth grade hallway, Savannah

stopped to wait for the others. When she glanced back, she froze. Allie was walking next to Jake, her expression full of excitement. She was talking nonstop…with her talented, dainty hand encased in his large, work-roughened one.

"Allie, lead the way," Savannah said, motioning for her daughter to precede her. She stepped in front of Jake to separate them as Logan followed his sister. Yet the image of Allie with Jake was burned into Savannah's mind and she had trouble concentrating on her daughter's explanation of the undersea drawing before them. Some long-buried part of her heart warmed to the sight of father and daughter together—something she'd never thought she would witness.

Reality crashed in on her a few minutes later just as Allie led them to her last picture. Michael was heading down the hallway, straight for them. He glanced at Jake and she could tell the instant her ex recognized him. His step faltered slightly, and his face revealed the sock to the gut he must be feeling. He gaped at them, his eyes moving between Jake and Savannah, as if trying to gauge how close they were.

"Dad!" Logan ran to Michael, and though Allie was more subtle, she stood in front of her horse head drawing, beaming at him.

After hugging both kids, Michael focused on Savannah.

"Hi," she said. "You remember Jake Barnes." She gestured to him and met Jake's gaze. She couldn't read his expression but was relieved it wasn't smug.

Jake offered a hand and Michael shook it.

"What brings you back to town?" her ex asked. His tone was uneasy and not particularly friendly.

"Family business."

"How long have you been back?"

"Longer than I'd intended."

"You were with Savannah at the hospital," Michael said, as if just figuring it out. "The kids said you drove her to the E.R., but I didn't make the connection until now."

He wasn't happy with the connection. That much was evident. Savannah just hoped Jake didn't notice and exacerbate Michael's displeasure. She felt pretty certain her ex wouldn't make a scene here...unless provoked.

"I was lucky someone was around to help me out," Savannah said, not mentioning that if Jake hadn't shown up and scared the daylights out of her, she probably wouldn't have cut herself in the first place. "We've already seen the displays of both kids, so why don't you go back through with Logan and Allie? We can wait outside."

Michael barely had a chance to answer before Logan was dragging him down the hall.

"He hasn't changed much," Jake said.

"Come on." Savannah led him to the doors. "We have to talk about something." Preferably before the rest of the Salinger-Rundle clan arrived.

"Sounds like I'm in trouble." She didn't have to turn around to know he was smiling. "Are you going to punish me?"

He made the words suggestive, and a chill ran down her spine. She didn't let her reaction show, though, just ignored him.

Once they were outdoors, she walked down the sidewalk, away from the main entrance so they could have some privacy. Jake followed her as she'd hoped.

"First of all," she said as she faced him, "thank you for last night." She rushed through the words.

Jake chuckled. "It's been awhile since I've had a pretty woman tell me that."

She punched him with her uninjured hand. "I was a mess. I don't do well with—"

"Your own blood," he finished for her.

"You noticed."

"Yes, and felt reassured to find out you do have a weak side."

She looked up at him, prepared to lay into him for giving her a hard time, but the sincerity on his face stopped her short.

"I have lots of weak sides."

He nodded. "If you say so."

She sure as heck wasn't going to list them for him. "Second of all…"

"Here it comes," Jake muttered, still more amused than concerned.

"This is serious. Last night, Logan asked why you're around so much. He thought maybe it was because you liked me."

Jake smiled at that.

"It's not funny, Jake. What am I supposed to tell him?"

"What *did* you tell him?"

"That you liked the whole family."

He struggled—unsuccessfully—to erase his grin, and Savannah stomped her foot.

"Cut it out, Jake! This isn't a joke. We're talking about my children. You think you've seen my bad side, but you haven't seen anything until you hurt my kids."

"I'm not hurting anybody, Savannah." He clasped her upper arms gently and forced eye contact. "Relax. Strange as it may sound, I care about those kids. Both of them."

She didn't fight him physically—she was too wiped out to struggle—but she met his gaze full force. "If you care about them, then back off."

"Can't."

She'd suspected he would say that. She sighed as a heavy wave of fatigue and worry and all the emotions from the past twenty-four hours engulfed her. "You can't visit them again before you leave. This is it."

"And when I return?"

"Savannah!" Her sister Katie called from down the sidewalk, and Savannah pulled away from Jake.

She moved around him and watched as her entire ever-loving family headed toward them. Katie and her fiancé, Noah. Lindsey, Zach and the boys. And to top it all off, her dad and stepmom.

Shoot me now.

Automatically, she tried to distance herself from Jake but he stuck right with her.

"It's a banner day," she told him quietly. "The whole family."

Zach greeted Jake first and shook his hand. Savannah introduced her sisters, Noah and the kids next, Billy and Owen, the nine-year-olds he and Lindsey had adopted. Then her dad and Claudia.

"Jake is...an old friend. We went to high school together."

"Ooh," Katie said, as if she just made the connection that this was *the* Jake.

Savannah shot her a subtle evil eye.

"Pleasure to meet you," their dad, Wendell Salinger, said. "You still live around these parts?"

Jake explained his log home business in Montana and his current work with Zach, and the men gravitated together to discuss Heartland's development project.

"Boys," Lindsey hollered at her sons, who were racing to the playground farther down the school yard.

"I'll watch them," Claudia offered. "Let 'em run some energy off before we herd them inside."

"If you don't mind," Lindsey said.

"Rough job, taking care of my grandboys." Claudia grinned and hurried after them.

"So…" Katie said quietly. "Jake, huh?"

"Don't get all coy and speculative on me," Savannah murmured. "You know who he is and what role he plays."

"Uh-huh. What I didn't realize is that he looks like *that*."

Lindsey surreptitiously glanced at him and nodded. "He's grown up quite nicely."

"It's not like that, and you guys know it. Can't be."

"Crying shame," Katie said.

"Now my evening is complete," Savannah groaned as she noticed Michael and the kids coming out of the school.

"You were supposed to wait for us to go inside," Lindsey said.

"I'd planned to, until we found Jake waiting for us at the door. Plan B was to get him out of here before you guys—and Michael—showed up."

"You should bring him to the wedding as your date," Katie said, not paying any attention to their discussion.

"Katie. The point is to keep him *out* of my life. I'm going to drag him away from Dad and Zach now, shove him toward his motorcycle and drive my kids home."

"That doesn't sound nearly as fun as the alternative." Katie laughed, but when Savannah didn't, she said, "Okay. Touchy subject. I get it. Let's go look at some kid art, shall we?"

Savannah didn't get much of a chance to talk to Jake alone again before they left. He walked them to the van and the kids got in and buckled up. Savannah waited outside the driver's door.

"What we talked about before…"

"I'm leaving Sunday, Savannah."

"Good."

"But I'll be back the week after. I'll get in touch with you then because I do intend to…" he peered in the window at the kids, then back at her "…be around them."

He sauntered off, and Savannah got into her van and slammed the door.

CHAPTER ELEVEN

Y EARS AGO, Savannah wouldn't have been caught dead at home on a Friday night. Funny how life, two kids and a divorce changed things. Now Fridays were her refuge, her favorite night of the week, whether the kids were home or not. She loved the solitude and the time that she didn't allow herself to do any work of any kind. It was her Friday rule. She could only do things she wanted to do, whether that meant watching television, renting a movie or curling up with a book.

Tonight, Logan was at a sleepover with one of his friends from school. She'd convinced Allie to play a game of Sorry! with her before her daughter had gone off to the room she and Logan shared to be alone. It wasn't much, but it was a step. Savannah knew she could only fight Jake off for so long. Eventually, Allie would learn the truth about him, and then who knew how it would affect their mother-daughter relationship. Savannah hoped to build it up as much as possible before that happened.

After Allie's retreat, Savannah caught most of a movie on TV. Halfway through, it hit her that she'd seen that film with Jake, as part of a large group of kids in high school. He'd made a point of sitting next to her to drive her crazy, and she realized tonight how much of the plot she'd missed because of his nearness back then.

She shrugged and got up off the couch. The movie was mediocre, anyway.

It was almost eleven. She'd told Allie good-night an hour ago, and now the place seemed quieter than usual. She headed into her bathroom, shed her clothes and turned on the shower.

Once under the hot spray, she allowed her mind to wander, urged her body to relax. The heated water steamed up around her, cutting out the chill of the day and warming her to the core.

As the shower slowly loosened her muscles, she tried to stop the rat race of her thoughts. Her brain sometimes exhausted her, but it was just part of who she was. Always analyzing, worrying, planning or figuring. She'd started making an effort to step away from thinking lately just to protect her sanity.

An image appeared in her mind's eye, a face with a sharp brown-eyed gaze and a slight smile. Almost a smirk. Jake's face. And the rest of him. She fully realized that allowing her brain to go in this direction was a bad idea, but she was tired. Lonely. Weak. So she let herself imagine what it would be like if she did let loose and said to hell with doing the right thing. What if she gave in to the desire she couldn't deny Jake made her feel?

Her eyes closed and her head rolled back slightly as she imagined what having Jake's naked body up against hers under the hot, steamy water would feel like. A heavy ache settled between her legs and the pounding of the water on her nipples put every nerve on alert, waiting for his touch.

Savannah opened her eyes suddenly when she realized her breathing was shallow and full of need. Not want. *Need.*

Jeez.

What was she thinking? She didn't *need* anyone, especially not Jake Barnes. She turned the faucet to cold, gritting her teeth against the shock to her system. Tension slid right back into every inch of her. But that was better than arousal.

Seconds later, she turned the water off, not bothering to shampoo her hair, even though she had wet it. She climbed out of the shower and grabbed her oversize bath towel, then wrapped herself in its warmth and illusion of security. Lowering herself to the bath mat, she sat there for several minutes, wrapped in her towel, scolding herself for letting Jake invade her mind.

Finally, Savannah rose and finished drying off, reminding herself that she was in control of her life and Jake wasn't part of it. At least not much. He definitely wouldn't be part of her showers.

After drying her hair most of the way, she went into her bedroom and pulled on her favorite pajamas—flannel bottoms with multicolored polar bears on them, and a long-sleeved thermal top. She slipped her feet into worn, fuzzy slippers and headed to the kitchen for a bedtime snack. As she switched on the kitchen light, a knock sounded on the door.

Her landlord definitely needed to spring for a damn peephole, she thought as she stood face-to-face with the subject of her shower fantasies. His hair was windblown. He wore a brown leather jacket that looked soft enough to sleep on, and dark jeans that hugged muscular thighs. His eyes were so intensely focused on her that she shivered.

In spite of everything she'd told herself in the past half hour, she couldn't deny the excitement that zipped through her at the sight of his smile. Couldn't deny it, but she *could* tamp it down and refuse to hang on to it.

"What are you doing here?" she asked, feeling exposed in her thin pajamas. She knew the top left nothing to the imagination.

Jake pushed the door open all the way and sauntered past her. "It's cold out there. Winter's close."

"October's like that in Kansas." She shut the door. "Keep your voice low. Allie's asleep."

He had the audacity to remove his jacket and lay it on the easy chair in the corner of the living room.

"I don't recall inviting you in," she said, stepping away from the door and the breeze that always seemed to penetrate the outer hallway. "Much less asking you to stay."

Jake slowly raked his eyes over her body, from embarrassing fuzzy slippers to frizzy damp hair and everything in between. Savannah crossed her arms over her chest as she felt her nipples coming to attention.

"About when I return from Montana…"

Savannah glanced toward Allie's bedroom door, but there was no sign of movement.

"The community center's having a party for kids on Halloween night. Tuesday that week," Jake said. "I'd like to take Allie and Logan."

Her mind spun as she tried to find a viable excuse to keep them away from him. Unfortunately, they had no specific plans for Halloween night, just a party at her sister's the weekend before. In fact, Savannah had already considered taking the kids to the community center.

Forgetting her attire, she uncrossed her arms and paced to the back of the couch. "It's too much. You've visited with them almost every day this week. Why can't you just be happy with that?"

"Why would I be? I've missed Allie's entire life because you didn't see fit to tell me about her. I intend to be part of it now."

"When it's convenient for you. When you happen to be in town. How do you suggest we explain your presence to the kids?" she inquired.

"Why do we have to explain anything?"

"Because they're asking. They don't understand what you're doing here, why you stop by and invite us to dinner."

"Why not just, 'Jake's a really nice guy'?"

"I make an effort to avoid lying to my kids whenever possible."

He advanced on her and Savannah stood her ground, but she immediately acknowledged the error of her ways when Jake's body pressed against hers, forcing her into the back of the couch. She raised her arms and placed her hands on his chest—which also turned out to be a mistake, because, wow, those pecs…

He smelled like worn leather and Jake, and her head swam with the familiarity. She knew full well her hands were there to provide a barrier, but she couldn't bring herself to push him away. She was caught in the spell of his closeness, their discussion forgotten.

His palms landed on her hips and his heat made her skin sizzle through the thin material of her pajama bottoms.

Their mouths were two inches apart, tops, and she felt his warm breath, mirrored his shallow, uneven breathing. His lids lowered and she knew he was staring at her mouth, knew it even as her eyes zeroed in on his mouth.

He leaned down and kissed her with lips that were demanding, lacking any gentleness, and Savannah met his urgency with her own. Their tongues touched and their hands grasped for each other, exploring. She ran the fingers of her uninjured hand over the muscles of his upper back, on top of his shirt, itching to feel his flesh.

He still had it—the power to turn her inside out with just a kiss. Judging by the moans that escaped from deep in his throat and the hardness that imposed on her lower abdomen, she could still make him dizzy with need, as well. Which just made the rush more intoxicating. Her mind ceased to function, her focus fixed on every sensation, every tingle and spark that seemed to shoot directly from her lips to her very core. She arched into him, slipping her hands under his shirt and clinging to his strong back, digging in her nails to pull him nearer.

He broke the kiss suddenly and tipped his head back, breathing hard, chin toward the ceiling. "Damn, woman."

Instantly incensed, ashamed and…*horrified,* she pushed him away. "I didn't start it…"

The corners of his lips quirked. "It wasn't that kind of 'Damn, woman.'"

"Oh." From the lustful look he was giving her, she realized he was saying, "*That was hot.*"

Which was an understatement.

But Savannah had been slammed back to earth when she'd read blame into his comment, and now she wasn't playing anymore. Instead, she was beating herself up, the heated flush and the lack of oxygen caused by this man still plaguing her, making her ache in places that had been numb for more than a year.

She moved a few paces to the right and stood with her back to him, hugging herself. "You think that if you kiss me, I'll let you take the kids on Halloween?"

"I think that if I kiss you, you *won't* let me take them. Why do you figure I stopped?"

She whirled to face him and stared at him in astonishment. *Common freaking sense, maybe?* She just shook her head.

Savannah made a beeline for the kitchen, hoping a glass of ice water would shock her system back into working order. How could she have lost her mind completely in two seconds flat?

Hoping for some space, she didn't bother to switch on the kitchen light. The big dense man followed her in. Savannah was holding her glass under the faucet when he came up behind her, gently lifted her hair and kissed her neck.

"Some women get boring when they get older, but you..." His whisper on her neck made her shiver. "You've got it all backward, honey. You're even sexier than you used to be."

The husky words heated her clear through. Just a simple statement, and an innocent kiss— No, scratch that thought. There was nothing innocent about that kiss. And the memory was all it took for desire to flare inside her again like a flame that kept a hot air balloon floating above the ground. She bit down hard and tightened her jaw, talking herself down.

"So." He'd helped himself to a glass and was filling it

with ice. His voice was perfectly normal. No sign of the throw-me-up-against-the-fridge-and-do-me passion it had dripped with just seconds earlier. "I'm pretty certain Michael figured out I know about Allie."

Savannah closed her eyes against the whiplash of not only the change in subject, but also the fact that he was fully recovered from their kisses and she was standing there wishing for a chair before her legs collapsed.

Bastard.

Focus, girl. Don't allow him any hint about what he does to you. You. Are. In. Control.

She absently cracked a knuckle as she shut the tap, took a long drink and turned toward him.

Now, what had he said? Ah, *Michael knows.* Yeah, that.

"What makes you believe he knows?" She was proud of her control when her voice emerged strong and normal instead of all…*needy.*

"A look he gave me. And a…vibe I got."

"A vibe." Okay. If he was unaffected, so was she. "A look and a vibe. You sound like a woman."

"You didn't seem to think that five minutes ago."

She felt the heat rise. "What do you think I should do about it?"

"You could kiss me again."

She set her glass down. "*About Michael.* What should I do about Michael?"

"That's your call, I'd say."

"Got that right. And I decide to do absolutely nothing."

"You don't think he'd get bent out of shape if I knew your secret?" Jake asked.

"He doesn't suspect. If he did, he would've said something." Savannah leaned against the stove, as far away from Jake as she could get in the small space. "Why does it matter if he knows that you know?"

Jake flashed that cocky grin. "It doesn't. Just thought you might want the heads-up." He hoisted himself onto the counter across from her. "What happened between you two, anyway?"

"Who two?"

"You never used to play dumb," he said, shaking his head. "Hubby dearest."

"*Ex*-hubby dearest." Savannah studied her fingernails. "He left me because I was too controlling."

Jake actually chuckled. "His words, I gather."

"Well, yeah, but it's true. In case you haven't noticed, that's the kind of person I am. I made him miserable."

Jake poured out the remaining water and ice and set his glass in the sink. "All these years I've known you and I had no idea you were controlling." He said it with a smirk.

"Why are you here again?"

"We were discussing Tuesday night. Halloween. Kids."

"No."

"You can go, too."

Spending more time with him was on her to-do list right after tearing off her fingernails one by one. "No."

"We agreed I could get to know Allie."

"You know her."

"Bullshit. Don't push me on this, Savannah."

She narrowed her eyes. He had just enough of a threat in his voice, and she was just enough worried that he would follow through on it that after a long while, she nodded. Barely. "Fine. Halloween."

"You'll have fun."

"I seriously doubt it."

"Lighten up."

"What *are* we going to tell the kids, Jake? Why are you hanging around us like a hungry puppy who got a bone once?"

Jake gazed at the ceiling, exasperated. He didn't get what the big deal was. Why everything had to be explained. Chances were Logan had forgotten the question as soon as he'd asked it.

"Tell them we're getting married," he said.

It was the wrong thing to say. That was clear from the frown on Savannah's face.

"I am never getting married again." She emphasized every word to make sure he got the point.

He got it.

"Joke. Down, girl. You think I want to wake up next to you every morning for the rest of my life?"

The image that flooded his mind as soon as he uttered the words was…alluring as hell, actually. Savannah in some drapey see-through lingerie, waking up slowly as he lay next to her, watching. Waiting. Ready to sate them both.

Every day.

For the rest of his life.

The idea didn't really suck. For a guy who'd never planned to get married himself, and who had a boatload of other problems to work out, that was saying something. Something he didn't care to ponder.

"And why aren't you getting married again?" Not that he was honestly considering marrying her.

"I'm too controlling."

Her reply was a cross between flippant and threatening, although Jake didn't feel the least bit threatened.

"Nah," he said. He and Savannah would never have the problems she and Michael had had because Jake would never lie down and take it.

No. He and Savannah would never have the problems she and Michael had *because they would never get married*.

CHAPTER TWELVE

JAKE WASN'T SURE WHAT to expect when he laid eyes on his dad today. Dean had gone noticeably downhill between Jake's first visit and the night he and Savannah had stopped by. There had only been a week between those occasions.

Jake didn't slow down as he got to the door of his father's room. He'd done plenty of hesitating earlier, but Emily had convinced him this might be his last chance to talk to their dad. Jake was going back to Montana tomorrow and wouldn't return to Lone Oak until Friday, when he would finalize the deal with Zach. His grandma had insisted on putting Jake's name on the agreement, as well, in case anything happened to her.

"Jake," his dad said in a steady, strong voice when he entered the room.

"Dad." He pulled up a chair near the head of the bed, relieved to see him so alert. "How you doing today?"

"Not too bad. Haven't had to have as much morphine." He looked better than he had on Monday, just five days earlier. He seemed more alert. His eyes focused better, his coloring was not so pale, and his speech was clearer, more confident.

Jake nodded. He leaned his elbows on his knees and

tried to think of something to talk about. What, exactly, did you say to your father during possibly your last conversation ever? Pressure built in Jake's head.

"Been doing a lot of thinking lately," his dad said. "Guess that's normal when you're in the position I'm in."

"I suppose it is. What have you been thinking about?"

Dean turned toward the window and stared out at the changing leaves. The trees were showing off yellows, oranges and reds bright enough to rival any sunset.

Jake watched as his dad's expression saddened, couldn't ignore his almost translucent skin. Once again he found it hard to believe this was the hearty man who used to let nothing slow him down, let nothing get in the way of his work.

"Rennie."

The single word, his mother's name, made Jake's head pound even more, and something in his chest catch. They had never really discussed her and what she'd done. Jake wasn't altogether sure he wanted to now. But he waited for his dad to say more. If a dying man wanted to talk about something, the least Jake could do was listen.

Dean relaxed his neck and rested his head back against the raised mattress. He finally spoke.

"I've never forgiven her. All the years since she swallowed too many pills, and I've held on to the anger." He shook his head slowly, then met Jake's gaze with watery eyes. "I've let it eat me up, become a part of me."

"I was mad at her, too."

"Tough not to be. But I should've gotten over it. Should've forgiven her. Instead, I became fixated on how her suicide affected me, what it did to make my life worse.

Hell, I didn't know what to do with you kids. I didn't know how to manage the home. Your mother handled all that."

"She did everything." She'd done it to a fault, too. The house had always been spotless. Meals cooked every evening, kept warm on the nights when his dad worked late. Jake had sometimes wondered if the complete lack of support from her husband had contributed to his mother's inability to keep on living.

"And I let you handle everything after she was gone, because I was too busy being mad." Dean was quiet for a long moment, gazing at the ceiling, looking pained. "I told you the other day that I'm sorry, but that doesn't really scratch the surface."

Jake nodded. "I understand."

"I don't believe you do, Jake. I've never been one to focus on regret, but this is tearing me up." He paused again, fighting to maintain his composure. "I've wasted my life on being angry. I wonder…" He swallowed, then closed his eyes. "I wonder how things could've been different if I'd just forgiven her and moved on."

Jake regarded him as the words hit home. Pondering his youth, he wouldn't have to stretch his imagination to see his dad had been pissed at the world. Or rather, at his late wife. "Regret won't do anything for you."

"I know, but that doesn't stop me from thinking about your mother day and night."

"So have you forgiven her now?" Jake asked quietly.

His dad made eye contact. "I have. At last."

"How do you suddenly forgive someone you've been mad at for almost twenty years?"

The older man attempted a smile, but his face seemed out of practice. "Part of it is just making up your mind to do it. To let the issue go. I finally figured I couldn't do a damn thing about my wife taking her own life."

"Just like that?"

"It wasn't just like that, necessarily. I talked a lot with your sister. She told me how she got through it over the years, how she tried to understand what it must've been like to feel the way your mom did. Emily's the most forgiving of all of us, without a doubt. Maybe it's a female thing."

"Could be."

"Speaking of females, tell me about the one you had with you the other night."

"There's nothing to tell."

His dad stared him down. "I don't believe that for a minute. There was an awful lot of tension between you two."

Tension. Yeah, there was that. Always had been. "We've known each other forever."

Dean nodded, still watching him. "And?"

"I don't know what to say. That's about it."

"I could tell you two like each other."

Jake chuckled. "I don't know that *like* is the right word."

"No, there was more than that. You two have a fight before you came in?"

When didn't they? "We have kind of an ongoing disagreement."

"That's a shame."

"Probably, but that's the way it is."

"Maybe you could work through it."

"You don't know anything about it," Jake said with irritation.

"That's because you're not telling me about it."

"None of it matters, because ultimately I'll be going back to Montana and Savannah is staying here."

With our child.

Damn, leaving Allie after he'd just found her was going to be hard. He'd have to make a point of e-mailing and calling regularly. They had to tell her the truth before then, though; otherwise she would wonder why he paid her so much attention from across the country.

"You have a decent life out there?" his dad asked.

"I like it. I have a nice piece of land and I'm building my company up."

His dad looked at him tiredly, concern in his eyes.

"What?" Jake asked.

Dean shook his head. "Just don't want you to be as unhappy as I've been. I hope I haven't made you that way."

"What's to be unhappy about? I told you my life is good."

"I've told myself that same thing countless times."

He was *not* like his father. Would never let himself be.

Jake stood abruptly, then checked himself. He couldn't rush out of here, not tonight. He inhaled slowly. "Dad. I'm glad we talked. I'm...glad I came home."

"Me, too." Dean blinked, then smiled wanly. "Take care of yourself, Jacob."

Jake couldn't speak around the lump in his throat, so he put his hand over his father's bony one and squeezed gently. "I'll be back in less than a week."

His dad nodded, though neither of them could voice their fears that he wouldn't make it that long.

THE VIEW FROM JAKE'S DECK was killer. Mountains in the distance, green rolling hills in every direction, a picturesque stream in the valley. This was what had made him fall in love with Montana.

He leaned on the railing for a few minutes as he got his morning caffeine fix. He probably couldn't afford these few minutes—they were pushing hard this week, working overtime to get Clayton's house finished before their deadline. Weather predictions were for frequent, deep snows during the upcoming winter and Jake intended to have everything done before they had to break for the weather. Fortunately, snow hadn't slowed them down yet. His crew had done a hell of a job while he'd been gone, and that was thanks to his right-hand man, Scott Turgeon. Jake would give him a healthy bonus once this project was pulled off.

He finished his coffee and took the mug into the kitchen. The room was currently cramped and closed off from the main living areas, but Jake had plans to remodel just as soon as his finances loosened up a bit. They'd loosen up nicely with the completion of Clayton's home, but until he landed more big projects, he'd have to pace himself.

Ten minutes later he was in his truck on the way to the job site. Fortunately, it was only about thirty miles from his own property, so he was able to stay at his place. As he turned onto the main road, his cell phone rang. He pulled over because the signal in those parts often faded in and out.

When he clicked off the phone less than three minutes later, he had to stifle the urge to get out of the truck and dance for joy. *Holy shit.* It was the call he'd been waiting for, for what had seemed like forever. Tony Clayton had been pleased with their work so far and had passed on Jake's name to his rich friends. Martin Fredericks, an in-demand movie producer, would like to meet.

Jake couldn't wipe the grin off his face. This was it, the beginning of what he'd wanted to accomplish. All he had to do was sit down with Fredericks one on one and show him some of the plans they could modify for him. The guy was presold, thanks to Clayton, and was ready to move ahead. He'd mentioned hoping to break ground as early as possible in the spring.

Things were definitely improving. Jake's goals were within reach.

Once on the gravel road that led to the job site, he noticed four horses in a meadow to his left. Allie would get a kick out of them. One was almost identical to the horse in the drawing she'd given him the day he'd found out he was her father.

Suddenly, the twelve hundred miles between them made her seem a world away. He missed her and her brother. Sure, Jake was returning to Lone Oak this weekend—in fact, he'd left his motorcycle there and flown to Montana because he couldn't afford to waste the two days of driving each way—but that was only temporary. He was a long distance from his little girl. He thought about how much his sister had changed since he'd seen her, even though she was an adult. At her age, Allie would change even more rapidly, and he didn't want to miss a minute of it.

He glanced in his rearview mirror at the horses again. Allie would absolutely love it out here. He had enough land that he could get a horse. There was a barn on his property that was currently unused. It would just require some minor work.

His heart pounded faster as he thought about the possibilities. He'd been joking when he'd suggested marriage to Savannah, but maybe that wasn't such a bad idea. In fact, it sounded like a beneficial option for everyone. He'd have his daughter close, Savannah could work for his company if she wanted to, her kids could have horses and the whole outdoors as their playground. Montana was an excellent place to live, to raise a family.

He swallowed hard. Did he really think that? *Raise a family?*

He might not be used to the idea, but he *was* a dad. He was determined to be an involved dad, and that was hard from twelve hundred miles away.

As he drove into the job site, he knew exactly what he planned to do. He planned to convince Savannah to marry him and move to Montana. For certain, he had his work cut out for him, but he couldn't abandon his company now, and he couldn't stand to be so far away from Allie.

CHAPTER THIRTEEN

SAVANNAH KNEW JAKE WAS in the conference room. Zach had told her they were signing the final paperwork for their deal today. Savannah had been picking up her kids when he would've arrived. Now she was hyperaware of the voices that carried out to the main office. Every once in a while she heard Jake's laugh, and she tried to ignore it.

The truth was she'd thought about him too much during the week he'd been in Montana. The kiss they'd shared the weekend before had done a number on her, even though she'd reminded herself repeatedly that it had been nothing but an accident. Chemistry did not make a relationship. Nor did she want it to.

The laughs were louder and nonstop now, as if the group was finishing up the meeting. Savannah glanced at the kids, who were on the floor between the desks, then busied herself and pretended she couldn't care less that Jake was there. The conference room door opened and her traitorous eyes zoned in on it.

Zach, the lawyer who'd drawn up the agreement, Mrs. Levine and Jake emerged, all of them smiling and joking, clearly happy with the deal they'd just sealed. Jake's gaze sought out Savannah, and she had trouble looking away.

Those brown eyes of his crinkled at the corners, drawing her in, and his smile was the real one, the one that could knock her flat.

She forced her attention to the bills she was paying on her computer.

"It's official," Zach said to her. "The Colonial Acres development is on its way."

Her brother-in-law beamed, appearing happier than he had since his wedding day. Savannah couldn't resist standing and giving him a hug of congratulations. This was big for him, for Heartland. He'd had other projects since he'd opened the company, but this was the largest by far.

As she released Zach, she caught Jake watching her with a certain expression in his eyes, as though he wanted *his* chance to wrap his arms around her. She shivered and turned her focus to Odessa Levine.

"Congratulations to you," she told the older woman. "It sounds like you have some unique ideas for the development."

Mrs. Levine grasped her hand and smiled. "Thank you. I certainly hope everything will work out. Jake and I have put a lot of thought into the plans. I can hardly wait to see the finished neighborhood."

"Did I hear you're going with a colonial style for all the houses and buildings?"

"You did. I think it'll go nicely with my little house. I sure am happy we could build around it."

Savannah smiled, then accidentally glanced at Jake again, who smirked as if sensing her discomfort.

"Where're my congrats?" he asked.

"Congratulations." She offered her hand instead of a hug.

When he accepted it, the contact had just as much of an impact on her as if he'd drawn her into his arms. He held on longer than necessary. Savannah became conscious that Zach was paying too much attention to them, and pulled away.

"We're heading to the Lazy Goat for a celebratory drink. I'd ask you to join us, but…" Zach nodded toward Allie and Logan, who were involved in a drawing and a video game, respectively.

"That's okay. I've got a stack of things I'm trying to finish here, anyway. Have a drink for me."

"We'll catch you tomorrow night at the party, then," Zach said.

She nodded, and couldn't help noting how patiently Jake helped his grandmother out the door. There was something about a man as sexy as him doing something so caring and attentive. He'd be a lot easier to dislike if he were mean to old ladies.

IT WAS STILL EARLY ENOUGH on Friday afternoon that the Goat was dead. When Zach, Jake and his grandma walked in, only two tables were occupied.

"You're supposed to be working, Zach," the short, blond bartender called out. The woman was maybe a few years older than Jake and had a toughness about her, although she was perfectly at home here and could handle whatever came up, be it a bar brawl or a drunken four-hundred pounder.

"Work related," he said. "Tough job. Kind of like standing around pouring beer for a living."

"Hey, don't mess with the woman in charge of the alcohol."

Jake accompanied his grandma to the first booth against the wall. "This okay?" he asked.

"As long as I don't have to slide far," she answered.

He helped her lower herself onto the bench seat. When he'd invited her to join them, he'd been shocked she'd said yes. He was glad she had, though. She didn't get out nearly enough to satisfy her active mind, and he knew the isolation would be worse once he left again. Emily tried to visit her weekly, but that still meant Odessa was alone most days.

"What's your poison?" he inquired.

"I think some champagne is in order, don't you?"

Jake glanced doubtfully at the bar. "We'll see what they have. I'll be back."

He went up to the bar next to Zach, who was still trading insults with the bartender. "The lady would like some champagne."

"What do you have, Heather?" Zach asked.

"I happen to have some very decent bubbly in the back. How much you want to spend?"

"As long as the stuff doesn't taste like toilet water, I don't care. Within reason," he said, as she headed to the back room.

Zach sat on a stool to wait. "Your grandmother is a hell of a woman."

Jake chuckled. "More so than I realized." He glanced over at their table. "She's getting into the trivia."

TVs hung throughout the bar, and some of them were set to the trivia channel. His grandma had found the control box on the table and was attempting to figure out how to operate it. He stifled his grin and went to help her.

Zach returned to their table a few minutes later. "We don't get the table service here but she did manage to locate some decent stuff." He set down three champagne flutes and filled each one. "Here's to a successful, prosperous partnership and to making Colonial Acres the best place to live in Lone Oak."

They clinked their glasses and sipped.

"You're right about this. It's not bad champagne." Jake's grandma took another sip and edged her glass aside. "Now I'm going to figure out how to use this machine, because I happen to be a trivia queen."

"I'm sure that's due to reading so many books," Jake said.

"Got that right. I'd challenge you any day."

Zach moved around the table to stand next to her, and explained which buttons to hit and how the game worked.

"It said I could play against people in other places. Is that correct?" she asked.

"It is."

She nodded intently. "You boys go play pool or some-thing. I've got a game to win."

Jake struggled not to laugh. "We'll be at the pool table." He swallowed a large sip of champagne, grimaced involuntarily and stood.

They stopped at the bar and Jake ordered a beer. "Never acquired a taste for champagne," he admitted.

"Wager?" Zach inquired on the way to the pool table.

"Why not? Twenty bucks." Jake selected a cue from the rack on the wall.

Zach racked and Jake broke in silence. He shot three stripes in and then missed.

Zach stepped up to the table and aimed. "So tell me something," he said as soon as he hit the one ball into the far corner. "What's going on between you and my sister-in-law?"

Jake was glad he wasn't shooting when Zach asked, because he would've missed. "What makes you think something's going on?"

Zach went for the three ball and then straightened. "I know Savannah pretty well. You send her into all kinds of strangeness."

Jake grinned at that. "Ya figure she likes me?" he questioned in a joking tone.

"Haven't decided between that and hate." Zach finally missed a shot and Jake walked forward to catch up.

"You've pretty much summed up our relationship right there." He smacked the thirteen just right and watched it roll toward the corner pocket.

"Relationship," Zach repeated. "Interesting choice of words."

Jake missed his next shot.

"Not sure what to call it." Jake studied Zach, getting a little of the older-brother, don't-mess-with-my-sister vibe. "I've known her since kindergarten." He moved toward Zach and glanced around to make certain no one could hear. "You're going to find this out eventually, anyway. Allie is my child."

Zach had just taken a drink, and choked on the champagne. "If that's your strategy to win the twenty bucks, it's a damn good one."

Jake grinned. "Afraid not. *That* is the strangeness you sense between me and Savannah."

"Is this something her family is aware of?"

Jake guessed that Zach was wondering if Lindsey had kept Savannah's secret from him.

"She just told her sisters. Her ex is in on it, of course. But that's it."

"How long have you known?"

"Less than a month."

"Man, that's rough." Zach hit balls in on his next two shots. "So I wasn't imagining the buzz between you two."

"Buzz?"

"Attraction. Chemistry. Whatever you want to call it, it's pretty noticeable. Now what do you plan to do?"

"Thought I'd set myself up for some rejection and ask her to marry me."

Zach shot in the eight ball to win the game. He straightened and returned to where Jake stood, a grin on his face. "Sounds like a hell of an idea. Savannah could use someone like you in her life."

"Tell *her* that."

"I don't tell that woman anything."

"You do know her well."

"You figure she'll say yes?"

Jake replaced his cue on the wall and pulled out his wallet to give Zach his money. "Not without a lot of convincing. I can be very persuasive, though."

"I wish you all the luck in the world."

They headed back toward Jake's grandma, who was still engrossed in her game.

"Thanks. I'll need it."

CHAPTER FOURTEEN

"Wowza!" Lindsey stopped in the doorway of her bedroom on Saturday evening, decked out in her pregnant nun costume. "You are one hot mama, Savannah."

"Hell makes a girl hot." Savannah turned her attention from the mirror and her chest that was so…out there, thanks to the low-cut devil costume with the built-in push-up bra, and frowned at her sister. "It's a good thing you're with child."

"Why's that?" Lindsey fluttered into the room with exaggerated innocence.

"Because I would hurt you if you weren't. What were you thinking when you got me this costume?"

Lindsey put her hands on her protruding belly. "If I had the choice between looking like you in that costume or looking like me in mine tonight, I'd be all over the slinky red pants and camisole. I feel like an elephant."

Savannah stood back and evaluated Lindsey. She picked up the nun's veil, which Lindsey had left on the bed while she handled last-minute preparations for her and Zach's Halloween party, and arranged it on her sister's head. And laughed.

"It's perfect! You'll be the comic queen of the party. I still think Zach should've gone as God."

"He didn't want to give Gram a heart attack."

"What kind of a day is she having?"

"Fairly lucid compared with the past week. She won't wear a costume, though. Annie got her Little Red Riding Hood, but she refused. Adamantly."

Savannah smiled, imagining the scene between Zach's grandma and her caretaker. Grandma Rundle was a lot mellower than she used to be, but the woman could still be stubborn and feisty.

Glancing back at the mirror, Savannah instantly forgot her amusement. "Lindsey, seriously, I can't go downstairs with this much of me showing."

"Don't be such a prude. You look fantastic. The dark red with your hair and coloring, your long legs and that cleavage…" Lindsey whistled. "You're a single woman and it's okay to act like one."

"I'm a thirty-one-year-old mom, not a hooker."

"Tonight, you're a devil." Lindsey gave her a smug, devil-may-care grin and spun to check her own appearance in the mirror. She frowned. "And I'm a dowdy woman of God."

"Maybe I could tempt you to come over to the dark side." Savannah stared pointedly at her sister's tummy. "Oops. You already have." She cracked up as she grabbed her cape, horns and pitchfork and hurried from the room, out of the pregnant woman's reach.

Lindsey caught up to her on the stairs.

"Are the kids okay?" Savannah asked.

"They're in the basement, playing haunted house. They have the lights off and are taking turns scaring one another. The babysitter will be here any minute."

"Going to have to tip her well tonight."

Once in Lindsey's kitchen, Savannah drew her thin, sparkly cape around her shoulders and attached it with the single snap. She wished it covered more than her back.

Grandma Rundle sat at the kitchen table, tapping a finger. She regarded Savannah for the longest time, assimilating the whole getup. Savannah braced herself for a too-honest remark. Now that the Alzheimer's had moved in on the woman's brain, she held her tongue even less than she used to.

"Pretty," she said instead.

Savannah gazed at her in surprise. "Don't you mean trampy?"

She shook her head. "You've got the figure for it, missy. Enjoy it while you can. One day you'll be begging for one of these jobs." She motioned to the sack-like pink-and-violet muumuu she wore, and grimaced.

"You never know. You might catch yourself a bachelor tonight with that 'job.'"

"I certainly hope not. Where's your man, young lady?"

"He's missing out."

Some days Grandma remembered Savannah was divorced now, but those were fewer and further between. She glanced at Annie, who nodded slightly, reassuring her it was okay not to go into the whole explanation again.

"What remains to be done?" Savannah asked Lindsey.

Her sister launched into a detailed list, ticking each item off on her fingers. She stopped midsentence and laughed.

"What's so funny?" Savannah inquired.

"The horns." Lindsey pointed at her headband. "They're absolutely perfect. The whole costume is."

Savannah pivoted to the counter and reached for the closest bottle of red wine, which Zach had opened earlier. "I'll just have a nice refreshing glass of wine. Would you like some— Oh, wait. You can't have any." Savannah shot Lindsey a grin worthy of the devil costume.

"Witch."

"Not tonight." She cackled evilly and began arranging the relish tray.

"Whoa." Zach, decked out in a hooded brown monk costume, gasped when he entered the kitchen. "You look like a woman on the prowl."

Savannah sighed. "I'm a woman at the mercy of your wife. I may still go change into a ghost with blue jeans."

"Don't you dare," Zach said. "Gram, Annie, can I get you ladies a drink?"

They both declined, but Grandma Rundle requested some of the sweets she'd seen Lindsey carry to the dining room earlier.

Savannah studied Zach, still puzzled by his comment. "Since when do you care what I wear?"

He shrugged guiltily and Savannah glanced at Lindsey.

"What did you guys do?" Then she knew. Or at least suspected strongly. "You invited your new partner, of course."

"Of course. I couldn't *not* invite him."

"And Lindsey told you everything…." She kept her voice down to avoid having the other women overhear.

"Not Lindsey," Zach answered. "I pried it out of the man himself. But as far as you and Jake needing to jump in the—" he broke off, eyeing his grandma "—needing to get together, I don't have to be up on any history to deduce that the jumping is overdue."

"You know he makes me crazy, right?"

"A little crazy never hurt anybody." Zach grinned.

Savannah felt her face start to flush, and not from embarrassment. "You guys don't understand. I can't go there." People acted as if she shouldn't think twice about finding another husband. How could she ever do that when her first marriage had done so much damage? She was not cut out for life sharing.

She took a large gulp of wine, made a face, then carried the relish tray to the table in the dining room, where the food was being laid out.

So Jake would be here. Great. She decided then and there to have a fun evening in spite of his presence.

Kelly, the babysitter, arrived, and Savannah escorted her down to the kids. The four of them were already wound up, as though they'd had nothing but sugar for a week. She kissed her children and told them all to behave themselves.

When she went back upstairs, guests were already arriving. Her instinct was to hang out in the kitchen with Gram and Annie.

Criminy. She'd never been afraid of people or mingling. Had never been a wallflower. She tried telling herself her reticence was due to the costume's neckline, which really had nothing to do with her neck at all it was so low.

"Better go find your man," Gram said, as if Savannah's thoughts were written all over her face.

Of course Gram had no idea what she was wishing on her.

The back door opened then and Katie and Noah walked in. Their home was next door and they'd only had to cross the backyards.

Savannah went over and hugged her sister. "Thank goodness you're here."

Katie tilted her head in confusion. "How much have you had to drink? You're never affectionate."

Savannah ignored her and stood back to admire their costumes. Noah wore a white jacket and carried a black bag. Katie had on a ski jacket, a stocking cap pulled down over her long hair, and fuzzy mittens. "Slip out of your coat so I can see what you are."

"My coat's part of the costume. I'm a mountain climber." A goofy grin stole over Katie's face as she grasped her fiancé's hand. "Noah's a medic, so he can save my butt when I fall off the side of a mountain."

"It doesn't count when you dress as your profession," Savannah said to him.

Noah stepped forward and kissed her on the cheek. "I'm a doctor. It's different. Besides, she needs to be saved."

"You already did that, honey." Katie wrapped her arms around his neck, a big grin on her face.

"You two make me nauseous," Savannah said, laughing.

"Who's here?" Katie asked, leaning down to hug Zach's grandma. "Where are my sweet niece and nephews?"

"In the basement. Though I'm not so sure about the sweet part."

Katie hollered down to the four and received overenthusiastic hellos back.

Lindsey arrived to get a round of drinks, and shooed them out of the kitchen.

"Sorry, Linds, not going to allow the preggo lady to do all the work. You promised you'd let us help," Savannah said.

"Fine." She fished out two beers and handed them to Savannah. "These go to the cowboy and the Hell's Angel in the living room."

"Cowboy and Hell's Angel," Savannah repeated.

As soon as Savannah reached the doorway, it became apparent Lindsey was inherently evil, in spite of her nun's costume. Jake was the Hell's Angel and Doug, one of the crew at work, was the cowboy.

Jake's lustful grin as she approached him incited chills. Absolutely annoying chills.

"If this is what the devil looks like, then line me up for hell," he said when she handed him one of the beers.

"As if you have any choice at this point," Savannah replied.

"Oh, she got you there, man," Doug said.

"Your costume is fitting," Savannah told Jake, checking him out from head to toe. Fitting very nicely, she might've added if it wouldn't have pained her to admit it.

Heat rushed through her at the sight of the black leather hugging those thighs. She'd never had a leather fetish, but he could give her reason to start. He wore what appeared to be a genuine Hell's Angels black jacket, with the words and a graphic on the back.

"Where'd you get that?" Savannah queried. "Tell me you're not…"

"I'm not. It's a long-lost uncle's. Emily found it when we were going through our dad's closets the other day."

Savannah nodded. "I better go help my sister with drinks."

Jake raised his beer can in salute.

When she pivoted around, Katie was in her face with a

cat-ate-the-canary grin. "He looks mighty fine tonight, doesn't he?" she whispered.

Savannah snarled at her and walked by, taking a couple of drink orders on her way to the kitchen.

JAKE WASN'T MUCH OF A party guy anymore, but the Rundles' Halloween bash was decent. That had nothing to do with the amusing costumes or the tables crowded with food or the free-flowing drinks, and everything to do with being able to watch Savannah in that devil suit.

When she waltzed through the room in the sparkly low-cut top, snug pants and black heels that made her legs seem a mile longer than usual, his mind ceased functioning altogether. She'd been doing her best to ignore him ever since bringing that first beer out, yet whenever she entered the room, her eyes sought his. They'd dart away at once, as if she'd never tried to find him, but he spotted her looking every time. And every time, his blood pounded harder.

Jake had been shooting the breeze with some of the guys from Heartland, since he didn't know many others. But now he'd had enough tiptoeing around what he wanted. He headed to the kitchen, where he'd seen Savannah disappear again.

The room was deserted, but the rear door was open a crack. He went to it and squinted out into the darkness. Sure enough, she sat on the top step by herself, rubbing her bare arms with her hands. Her breath made clouds of white mist as she exhaled, and Jake imagined the warmth of it on his skin.

Enough imagining.

"Hey," he said, walking out and sitting next to her. "Cold much?"

"I wanted some fresh air."

"This is pretty fresh." He removed his jacket and draped it around her shoulders, on top of her cape. "I see your horniness has disappeared," he said, eyeing her hair where the devil headband used to be.

Savannah pulled the jacket tightly around her. "Don't worry. I'm still bad on the inside."

"And very good on the outside. Just the way I like 'em."

Instead of laughing, she sighed. "Jake, why did you come out here?"

He rested his elbows on his knees and gazed straight ahead at the mother-in-law quarters in the backyard. "You want honesty or some more lines?"

"What do you think?"

He took several breaths of cold air before speaking. "You're making me crazy, woman. I can't stop watching you, remembering us. I want…"

"You want what?" Her voice was hard, lacking any encouragement.

Jake was through waiting for encouragement, anyway. "This."

He put his hand on the back of her neck and drew her mouth to his, the warmth of her breath making him shudder with desire. She stiffened and didn't respond…for all of five seconds. When his tongue slid over her lips, she yielded to him and leaned closer. Jake trailed his hands up under the jacket, over the thin material of her top, then reached under it at her waist to touch her silky skin. Savannah made a soft, approving sound deep in her throat.

The noise of the party faded away and there was nothing except the two of them and the connection of their bodies, their mouths. Savannah worked her way up onto his lap and straddled him, and their hands were all over each other, grasping at clothing, exploring greedily.

Jake ran his palms under the silky material, up both sides of her rib cage, and rubbed his thumbs over the swells of her breasts. As he worked higher and made contact with her nipples, Savannah arched into him, exposing her neck. He pressed light kisses along her jaw. The little sounds she made nearly drove him mad. He dropped his hands to her backside and pulled her into his—

"Mom?"

Savannah shot to attention and stiffened. She instantly moved off him to return to her spot on the step, and tried to act as if she hadn't been busted in the middle of one extremely hot moment. It was a good thing they'd been interrupted when they had, Jake thought, because he'd been on the verge of losing the last thread of control.

"What's up, Allie? Is Kelly okay?"

"Were you kissing him?"

Savannah's head dropped. "Apparently so."

Tension filled the silence. Jake closed his eyes, aware that Allie wasn't okay with what she'd witnessed.

"Allie? Was there a problem in the basement?" Savannah asked.

A petulant sigh came from behind him. "The boys keep making us watch boy movies."

"I thought you would each get to choose a show."

"But mine was a long time ago."

"Whose show is on now?" Savannah asked.

"Billy's. He's making us watch Power Rangers. They're stupid."

"Can you go to the other side of the room and work on a new drawing?"

"It's dark. They're playing 'movie theater.' Creeps."

Savannah sighed, and Jake could practically feel her digging deep for more patience. "Tell Kelly I said to let you turn on a light so you can draw."

"'Kay." Allie paused. "Are you going to kiss him again?"

"No." Savannah's tone said she meant it…or wanted to.

The girl stepped back into the house, letting the door slam.

SAVANNAH BLEW OUT A LONG breath of air and ran her hands through her hair. Clearly, Allie was upset about Jake. And because Savannah had had no intention of kissing him tonight, let alone getting caught by her daughter, she was completely unprepared to deal with this problem. Why had she succumbed?

She chuckled. She had succumbed because the attraction between Jake and her had the gravitational force of a small planet. Or something. She wasn't really up on science, and she definitely wasn't up on attractions.

"She'll be all right," Jake said.

He was either full of crap or clueless, but Savannah said, "Yeah."

"So I thought of a solution for the whole parent thing with the kids and you and me."

"And that would be?"

"Let's get married. You guys could move to Montana with me. Allie could have a horse."

Savannah closed her eyes and wondered if this day could get any worse, because so far she was still upright and maybe it would feel better if she wasn't. "You can't be serious, Jake."

"Serious as a heart attack."

Her eyes widened and she slowly turned her head toward him. "How much did you drink?"

"I'm sober. Promise."

"You're off your rocker."

"Why is my idea so crazy? We're her parents. We want the same thing—what's best for Allie."

"I don't grasp how me marrying you could possibly be beneficial for Allie."

"She gets a live-in dad, you get a co-parent, Logan gets a role model."

"What do you get, Jake?"

He stared straight ahead. "Come on, Savannah. It's the practical thing to do."

She suddenly started laughing, her shoulders shaking uncontrollably. She didn't even know what was funny, or if anything was. Yet all she could do was sit there and laugh until tears filled her eyes. Then it struck her that these were not tears of joy. They were the real McCoy.

She wiped her eyes with the Hell's Angel sleeve and inhaled a steadying breath, except it turned out anything but. "Jake."

"Savannah."

"Why would I marry someone who holds a grudge against me?"

"What grudge is that?"

"The one about missing out on eleven years."

Jake seemed to give that some thought. "Might take me awhile to get over it, but I will."

"Marriage is not practical, grudge or no grudge. It's anything *but* practical." She lay back on the concrete landing outside the door, gazing at the stars, feeling so darn tired.

Jake bent toward her and whispered, "Totally…practical."

He kissed the sensitive spot beneath her ear, then stood and went inside, letting the door slam just as Allie had. Like father, like daughter.

The tears instantly reappeared in Savannah's eyes, and now she let them fall.

CHAPTER FIFTEEN

"GUYS, I'M PREGNANT, not dying," Lindsey said when everyone but her sisters had left the party. "And I'm not letting you ruin my kitchen." She got up from the ladder-back chair Zach had banished her to, and walked over to the counter. "These go in the dining room hutch." She took the crystal serving dishes Savannah had just dried, and headed for the front of the house.

"Zach's going to blow a gasket when he sees her cleaning up again," Katie said.

"She's a big girl. She can handle it and him." Savannah rubbed another piece of pain-in-the-butt, non-dishwasher-safe china dry with a now-damp towel.

"I noticed you disappeared from the party for a while," Katie said.

"Wanted some air."

"Uh-huh. For as long as you were gone, you must've nearly frozen with just the devil costume."

Savannah eyed her sideways and could tell Katie knew Jake had joined her outside. She didn't rise to the bait.

"Imagine my surprise," Katie continued, "when soon after, I saw Jake without his jacket."

"Yeah? He joined me. So?"

"Did he *join you* join you?"

Savannah could play games with her sister all night, but who had the energy?

"He asked me to marry him."

The heavy pan Katie had been scrubbing sloshed back into the water and clunked on the sink bottom. She slapped the spigot off and stared at Savannah. "I'm going to assume this is another one of those things you wouldn't joke about."

Savannah couldn't help laughing. Not the same hysterical shakes of earlier, but an evil, I've-succeeded-in-wigging-out-my-sister howl. She nodded her head in response to Katie's statement.

"And you said?"

"You have to ask? Really?" Savannah turned the water back on to rinse a serving bowl. "Well, I never really answered, if you want to get technical. But I'm pretty sure he got the implied 'Hell no.'"

"Linds!" Katie called to the other room. "Get in here. *Now.*"

"I can handle myself when Zach explodes," Lindsey said as she made her way back into the kitchen.

"We know you can. Sit down." Katie led her by the elbow to a chair.

"You people are making me crazy, you realize that?"

"Jake asked Van to marry him."

Lindsey's eyebrows shot up and her eyes got as big as quarters. She looked at Savannah, then back at Katie, seemingly waiting for the punch line.

"We're going to Vegas next weekend," Savannah said.

If Lindsey's eyes could get bigger, they did. Katie hit Savannah lightly and said, "No way."

Savannah struggled to keep a serious face, but couldn't for long. "Apparently, *that* is something I will joke about," she finally said. "Are you guys nuts?"

"If I go into premature labor, it is totally your fault," Lindsey said. "You're serious about the proposal part? Jake really asked you to marry him?"

"My advice?" Noah said as he and Zach strolled in from the living room. They'd been out front talking to the last stragglers. "Elope."

"The sexy getup worked then, huh," Zach said.

"I'm not marrying him. Not marrying anyone, but thanks for the thoughts, guys."

"Pleasure." Noah bent over and kissed Katie on the lips, lingering until the rest of them told them to stop.

"Boys, go away," Lindsey said. "This is girl talk."

"Gladly," Zach said. "We're going to return the folding table we borrowed next door."

The men retraced their steps and Katie removed the dish Savannah was drying, placed it gently on the counter and led her to the table, then sat between her sisters.

"So you said no. How come?" she asked.

Savannah sighed. "It's so true what they say about once you fall in love you want *everyone* to be in love. Let's see. First reason, I'm not going to remarry. Second reason, *ever.* Third reason, marrying for the sake of a kid is the dumbest thing I've ever tried and failed at. That's just the beginning of the list. Care for more?"

Lindsey rested her hands on her nun tummy. "I hear you. But I don't agree."

"You think I should marry him? Are you high?"

"Not necessarily. I have no idea if Jake's the guy for

you, because I don't really know him. What I don't agree with is that you won't marry again ever. I don't get that."

"Me, neither," Katie said, leaning her chin on her hand and staring at Savannah as if she were a feature article in the making.

Savannah shrugged. "I'm not cut out for it."

"For marriage? That's ridiculous," Lindsey said. "Just because one failed doesn't mean you're not cut out for it."

"I'm not. Remember me? Ms. Controlling?" She shook her head. "I have no desire to give up any control, girls. I love control."

"At last she admits it," Katie said.

"I've always admitted it. What I never realized before was that it wouldn't work in a marriage." Savannah planted both elbows on the table. "Michael had every reason to take off. There was no partnership in anything. It was all me, all the time."

"You may have controlled everything, but you also handled everything. House, kids, life," Lindsey said. "He didn't have a bad gig, Savannah."

"Having someone wash your clothes and care for your children does not make a marriage."

Lindsey apparently had no reply to that.

"So…" Katie began. "Can we back up for a second? Was Jake serious about this proposal?"

Savannah slowly nodded. "He was. I keep going over the conversation, searching for a smirk or something I missed, but I believe that if I'd said yes, he would've gone ahead."

"And how did he take the rejection?"

"The way Jake takes everything. He walked away."

"Marrying him would solve a lot of problems," Lindsey mused.

"Linds. Shut up. He wants us to move to Montana." Savannah jumped up. "I have to pay Kelly and tell her she can leave." At the basement door, she glanced back at her sisters. "Not a word of any of this to Dad."

"Does he know about Jake yet?" Lindsey asked.

Savannah shook her head. "Nothing."

"You really have to tell him. If he finds out any other way…"

"I'm going to tell him. Soon," she promised over her shoulder, and then descended into the mostly quiet basement to kiss her children good-night for their sleep-over, and rescue the babysitter.

She'd tell him, just as soon as she could get up the courage, she mused. Confessing to her dad that she'd made some serious mistakes didn't top her list of Fun Things To Do Before She Died.

JAKE HEARD THE KIDS laughing and thumping around inside before he knocked on the door. Theoretically, they hadn't even begun the Halloween festivities yet. Just wait until he got them full of sugar at the community center party.

"Jake!" Logan was the one to open Savannah's door and drag him in, as if the party were there instead of on Main Street. He was covered from head to toe in black, including a hood and a belt full of plastic weapons.

"Hey, Mr. Ninja. Excited?"

Allie skipped over to him, her eyes shining. She wore her hair in two braids under a straw cowboy hat with a pink ribbon. A pink-and-gray-plaid shirt, jeans, and pink cowboy boots completed the costume.

"What have we here?" Jake asked. "Wait, let me guess. You're a scarecrow."

"No-o," Allie said with a laugh.

"She's a cowgirl!" Logan hollered.

"Ahh. I can tell now. You just need a horse."

"I asked for one for my birthday, but I didn't get it. Not a real one, anyway."

Savannah breezed in from her bedroom then, and Jake was momentarily disappointed she wasn't wearing the devil costume from the other night. She wasn't wearing any costume at all. Just dark jeans that hugged those long legs, and a fuzzy cream sweater. Her shoes were brown, bootlike things with heels that made her only a few inches shorter than him.

"I was hoping you'd have your costume on," he told her.

"This *is* my costume. I'm a single mom with her act together." She moved around the room, gathering up a couple of random toys and her purse as she spoke. "Notice I don't have a hair out of place," she said, pointing to her locks, which were straighter than he'd ever seen them and pulled back at her nape. "My outfit doesn't clash, I have matching socks, even though you can't see them..."

"And her underwear and bra match, too!" Logan said in his usual "outdoor" voice.

Jake laughed and Savannah looked like she might wring her son's neck.

"That's private," she scolded.

"Sorry," Logan said, slightly abashed.

"See?" Savannah addressed Jake. "Note that a frazzled single mom would've lost her cool there. I've got it together."

"Gotcha." The outfit was clever, but had nothing on the devil's cleavage. "Let's get going. Trunk-or-treating started ten minutes ago."

"Where's my pumpkin?" Allie asked, wandering in circles, searching for it.

"Your pumpkin?" Savannah queried.

"For her candy." Logan held up his big round Spider-man version of a candy toter.

Savannah frowned. "I haven't a clue. You had it before dinner. You were swinging it."

A full five minutes passed before they found it on the bathroom floor. Savannah was rushing around now, hunting for coats to throw over the kids' costumes as she tugged her own coat around her.

"So much for your costume," Jake said quietly as they followed the children out the door.

She sent him a phony grin. "We hadn't left the house yet. Doesn't count."

She led him to the garage below and lifted the old door by hand.

"I hope you don't mind driving," Jake said. "Didn't figure we'd all fit on the Harley."

"Mom always drives," Allie told him.

"Duh. She's the only one who's old enough," Logan said.

"She even drove when Daddy lived with us," Allie remarked authoritatively.

"I'm a better driver," Savannah stated.

Jake thought she might be partially joking, but he couldn't be certain. "I have a truck back in Montana," he said.

"Cool," Logan called from the middle of the van. "Is it one with a backseat for kids?"

"It is. Lots of room there."

He turned around from the passenger seat to find Logan nodding. "So me and Allie can fit in if you ever bring your truck here," the boy said.

Savannah eyed Jake before backing out. Instead of the killer glare he'd half expected, he got kind of a nervous, secret-sharing look. Was she reconsidering his proposal? Jake checked the urge to touch her hand reassuringly. Savannah was the last person who usually needed reassurance.

Two minutes later they entered the fray known as trunk-or-treating. The community center parking lot was packed with cars in every space, each with the trunk or rear doors open. People handed out treats to kids as they made their way from vehicle to vehicle.

Jake and Savannah walked behind Allie and Logan, keeping just out of the rush of children but close enough to stay in sight. When they hit the end of the first row and rounded to the next aisle, Jake slipped his hand around Savannah's.

"What are you doing?" she asked so no one else could hear. She didn't remove her hand, though.

"Excellent question," he said. "It could be answered a couple different ways."

"Such as?" Her eyes twinkled, even though she tried to act annoyed.

"Well, first you get the practical argument. I'm keeping your hand warm."

Her eyebrows rose skeptically and she fought a grin. "Or I could whip out a pair of thick mittens."

"You could. If you were really a single mom with her act together and had some with you."

"Touché. What's the other argument?"

"The nonpractical one."

"Which is?"

"Because I want to."

Savannah rolled her eyes.

"Some people would say that's not reason enough to hold hands, but clearly, it is. Because you want to, too."

"I do, huh?"

Jake nodded. "When two people want the same thing, it's often a good idea to go ahead with it." He craned his neck to locate the kids again, letting the words hang between them.

Allie spotted him watching her and ran over. When she noticed how close Savannah and Jake stood, and saw their interlocked hands, she glared at her mother and yanked Jake's other hand.

"Hey, Jake. Come with us to the next van. It's decorated all spooky."

He caught the frustration on Savannah's face before he was drawn more deeply into the crowd with Allie.

SAVANNAH WOULD *NOT* LET the absence of Jake's warmth bother her. She wouldn't get upset by her daughter's snub or chilly reception. Tonight was all about the kids, she reminded herself.

She hadn't meant to keep holding on to him, but the roughness of his skin in contact with hers, the way he'd gently caressed her with his callused thumb, had intrigued her, made her respond to him, made her cherish the touch. Made her want those hands to keep touching her. Everywhere.

Which put her in a quandary. Two quandaries, really.

When Allie so openly disapproved, Savannah was torn. Her instinct was to avoid letting her children interfere with her personal decisions. Her life was her own and she wasn't going to let an eleven-year-old run it. Unfortunately, things weren't so cut and dried. The eleven-year-old was one of the people Savannah loved most in the world, and whom she was on the verge of losing all semblance of a relationship with.

And then there was the whole gray issue of whether she wanted to fight for the right to hold Jake's hand. His smugness when he'd sidled up so close and wound his warm, strong fingers around hers had made her want to push him away and observe his reaction. But another part of her, the trouble-causing part, reveled in his aggressiveness, his confidence.

Allie would dislike her no matter what Savannah did. Regarding Michael, regarding Jake, regarding breathing. She couldn't please her daughter, couldn't do anything to win her back. She'd tried. Even expensive art classes had failed to give them something to talk about.

But somehow Savannah resisted letting Jake in on any aspect of her private life. That went so much deeper than her current volatile relationship with her daughter. It wasn't even that he'd proposed, because she felt confident she could refuse the marriage suggestion till the cows came home. The feelings were what she didn't like to handle. Or maybe couldn't. Because if she could fight them off, she would've swatted Jake's hand aside like a pesky West Nile-infected mosquito.

There it was again—that lack of control that always swept her away in Jake's presence. She stifled a growl, searching for Logan, whom she didn't immediately spot with Jake and Allie. There was his little clad-in-black head. She moved toward him.

As for control, she had to do better than she'd done so far tonight. For her kids to pick up her mixed messages to Jake wasn't fair. Because no matter how tempted she was, she would never have a permanent relationship with him or any man.

BY NO FAULT OF Jake's, he and Allie became a team. Savannah and Logan made their way around the indoor party activities separately. He would've loved that his daughter had chosen him and wanted to be with him, if it hadn't meant Savannah's being shafted by her own kid.

He figured that when they rejoined, Savannah would have words for him because he'd been alone with their child. But the crowd and Allie had taken him away, and he'd let them, not realizing how long they'd be apart.

Now Allie was throwing pumpkin beanbags at plastic vases, trying to win a prize. When her three bags were gone, she turned to Jake. "Next, the Plinko game," she said excitedly.

They stood in line for a few minutes, then she dropped a disk at the top of the board and watched it fall to determine her prize. Luck was on her side tonight; she won the top prize, a stuffed black cat.

"I have to go to the bathroom," she said as they moved away from the Plinko crowd.

Jake glanced toward the throng outside the main restrooms, then checked the other way, down a side hall. Spotting another bathroom, he held his hand out to Allie, then he wondered if she would take it or if she thought she was too old to hold a grown-up's hand. She hesitated, then grasped his fingers.

As he waited for her to come out of the otherwise deserted restroom, Jake skimmed the notices on a nearby bulletin board. When he saw the handwritten flyer about horses for sale, he smiled, and wished for once he was rolling in cash. Maybe one of these days. Money would likely be less of an obstacle than Savannah.

Allie appeared, grinning up at him and holding on to her stuffed cat.

"Why don't we go find your mom and brother."

The grin morphed into a frown. "How 'bout we try some more games?" she said.

He gently pulled her to the side of the hallway. "What's up with you and your mom tonight? I noticed the look you gave her outside…."

Allie crossed her arms and dropped her gaze.

Jake leaned down a bit to make eye contact, but attempted not to appear the bad guy. He was concerned about Allie's treatment of Savannah, yet his own relationship with the young girl was so new he didn't want to alienate her if he could help it.

"I gathered you didn't like me being with your mom the other night at the party."

"Or tonight," she offered.

"Your mom and I are friends. What's wrong with that?"

"Friends don't kiss."

She did have a point, but not one he would concede.

"I didn't kiss her tonight." Jake nudged her chin up a little with his thumb. "I like both of you, Allie. The three of you. Can't I be friends with all of you?"

Her brows knitted and she lowered her gaze again. "I'd like you to be *my* friend. I don't want my mom making you go away."

"What do you mean, honey?"

"She made my dad go away. I don't want her to do that to you."

Ah, hell. Jake stood up as he wondered how in the world to handle this. He'd like to reassure his little girl he wouldn't go away, but Savannah was a wild card and he couldn't be certain she'd let him continue to get closer. Yes, he would maintain ties with his daughter at all costs, regardless of what happened between him and Savannah, but as far as being a regular in the family's life…who knew what would happen. The one thing he couldn't do was promise Allie he and Savannah would always be on amiable terms.

He bent down again. "I'm not going anywhere. Even when I return to Montana in a few days, we can keep in touch. If you and I are friends, we'll continue to be friends, no matter what happens with your mom."

Allie shook her head. "She won't let us stay friends if she makes you go away."

"You still get to see your father, right?"

She chewed that over for a few seconds. "Yeah, but he's my dad. I have to see him."

Jake closed his eyes and bit his tongue to keep from telling her he was her dad, too, and that there would be no problem. How to convince her everything would be okay without telling her the truth?

"Allie, do you trust me?"

"I dunno. I guess so."

"Then try hard to believe it when I say everything will be okay. You are one cool kid. I like you and won't just disappear."

She sized him up in a way similar to her mother, and with a lot of effort, Jake maintained a straight face. Finally, she nodded.

"I still don't want to go find my mom, though."

Jake couldn't help smiling briefly. "Sorry, kiddo. She's your mom." He held out his hand. "But I'll be there, too."

CHAPTER SIXTEEN

JAKE FOLLOWED SAVANNAH to the kitchen after they'd put both children to bed.

"Don't go getting too comfortable, Barnes."

"Now I'm Barnes? I help tuck your kids in and we revert to last names?" He came up behind her, so close she felt his heat all along her back, from her thighs to her shoulders. "I figured that'd make you nervous." He reached in front of her and grabbed a handful of peanuts from the open can on the counter, then backed away. She cursed herself for missing his closeness.

She turned and glared at him, acting fiercer than she felt, and he grinned.

"I never said you could have some of my nuts, either," she said.

"I'll buy you new nuts, sweetheart."

Savannah dug out her own handful and faced him. "You and Allie sure disappeared tonight."

"Yeah." Jake dusted the leftover salt off his hands. "I wanted to talk to you about that."

A rock of dread filled her stomach and she pushed the peanut can away. Jake, typical man-who-could-eat-through-anything, took it from her and plucked more nuts out to pop in his mouth. She waited tensely until he finished chewing and got to his point.

"We have to tell her, Savannah."

She shut her eyes and resisted the urge to scream. "Jake. We've gone over it a hundred times. We're not telling her now."

"She needs to know. She's convinced you're going to make me go away."

"She's a wise little girl with a good idea," Savannah said dryly.

"Glad you can joke about the reason your daughter scowls at you more often than she breathes."

Savannah fought to swallow the hurt that rushed up her throat like bile. "You think telling her will make her run into my arms?" Her voice was a vicious whisper, kept in check by her stark fear of Allie learning the truth.

"She'll be angry, hurt—of course she will. But are you saying she's not both those things right now? You're deluded if you think offering her a chance to forgive you for the divorce, and then dropping yet another bomb on her, will work in your favor."

"So now you're an expert on family relations. How's it going with your dad?"

Jake flinched, as if she'd struck him physically. "I'm not an expert on family anything." His eyes met hers and held.

Dammit, why did she have to feel bad? Why, in the midst of his attacking her and threatening to throw her life so far off-kilter she didn't believe she could ever recover, did sympathy overcome her at his humble concession? She drew closer to him.

"He's still…alive?" she asked quietly, dropping their argument for now.

Jake nodded and straightened. "Wasn't sure he'd make it till I got back in town, but apparently, he rallied."

"Apparently? You haven't been to the hospital?"

"I saw him before I left."

"You have to go visit. Even if he rallied, he doesn't have much time."

"You sound like my sister."

"Wise woman."

"Something like that. Can we get back to Allie?"

"Go see your dad."

"If she learns the truth, she won't worry so much about losing me. About you making me go away."

"And tell him about his granddaughter. That'll show him you care."

"So now *you're* an expert on family relations?" Jake asked her pointedly.

Her shoulders sagged. "Touché."

Neither of them spoke for a long while. The refrigerator motor started up, filling the room with a comfortable buzz, but they just stood there, against the cabinets on the same side of the kitchen, inches apart, at an impasse. Or was it a temporary truce?

"Do you want to tell her before or after we tie the knot?" Jake inquired.

Definitely not a truce.

"You've been hallucinating if you think we're getting married."

Jake took hold of her hand and gently wove their fingers together. She couldn't seem to move away from his touch. His heat. The tenderness that she knew flowed through him.

She expected him to plead his case again, to argue with her why getting married was such a *practical* idea. Instead, his lids lowered halfway with barely controlled passion and his eyes zeroed in on her lips.

But he didn't kiss her right away. With his free hand, he brushed her hair behind her ear, tenderly, just a whisper of contact. Then he trailed his fingers along her jaw, making her crave more of his touch. Savannah leaned into his hand and, without conscious thought, kissed his palm, eliciting a sound from deep in his throat.

She ached for him to kiss her with all the desire she saw in his eyes, but still resisted. Pressing tiny kisses on his skin, she worked her way up his little finger, bit by bit. When her lips reached the tip, she caressed it with her tongue and drew it into her mouth to suckle briefly. Then she entwined their hands and pulled him flush against her body. Her lips parted, but, dammit, he still didn't make the final move to kiss her. Her breath caught in her throat as, winding her arms around the back of his neck, she inclined his head to hers, then finally touched that infuriatingly sexy mouth of his.

For all his refusal to initiate the kiss, Jake responded now and took over, his tongue roving, seeking hers, exploring frantically as if he expected her to retreat at any second.

Savannah wasn't stupid. The house could burn down around them before she'd end this soul-scorching, demanding kiss. Their hands roamed, discovered, found bare, hot skin beneath clothing.

He picked her up, never breaking the contact of their

lips, and Savannah wrapped her legs around him, wanting more of him, pressing her body against the unmistakable hardness in his jeans. Needy, breathy sounds filled the kitchen and she wasn't sure whether they were from her, him or both of them.

Jake eased her onto the counter. There, he unfastened her bra and cupped her breasts beneath her sweater, sending a pulse of electricity and desire even deeper to the center of her. She arched into him, gasping for air and release. His fingers worked magic over her nipples, making her crazy with need. She grabbed at his shirt and yanked it up, ready to strip him bare and have her way with him; in the kitchen, on the counter, on the floor—she didn't care.

"Damn," she said between hitched breaths, sliding his shirt back down.

"What?" His voice was ragged.

"Kids. Sleeping. Other room." She nibbled at his lips, lightly, attempting to separate herself from him and regain her sanity.

"Damn!" He breathed out shakily. "Crazy."

He kept kissing her with playful nips as well, as if he couldn't stop.

Savannah closed her eyes and struggled to pull in a full breath. Jake rested his forehead on hers and she could feel his heart pounding, or maybe it was hers. They were silent as they sought to regain their composure.

"If we got married, we could do this every night," Jake said huskily. "And more."

The thought of "and more" made Savannah shiver. She felt Jake smile, but she was still too jellylike to move. Or speak. And she really wished he'd stop ruining things by speaking, too.

"I felt that," he whispered. "You want me. You want to be with me. Why are you fighting it?"

There it was—the right motivation to snap her back to attention and quit with the clinging.

"Tell me you don't want me, Savannah. Tell me you're not still shaking from...*that*. Because I am."

She leveled her eyes at him and nodded. "Yeah. Got me there, Jake. I want you. Our chemistry has never been lacking." She stepped away from him. "But how can you possibly consider that enough for a marriage?"

He studied her, his eyes dark with heat. "You're still running, aren't you?"

"I've been here the whole eleven years you were gone."

Jake shook his head. "Eleven years ago *you* ran. You may have stayed in Kansas, but you pushed me away because you couldn't handle the way I make you feel. It scares the hell out of you."

"You should go, Jake. I don't have energy to fight this battle with you anymore. I'm not marrying you. I'm not marrying anyone."

She headed to the living room and opened the front door, but Jake didn't follow. She angrily retraced her steps to the kitchen.

"Leave. Please."

He gazed at her with eyes that seemed to see deep inside her, with an assumption that he'd been right on. He thought he understood her hesitancy. But she wasn't afraid of him. She just hated the way he made her common sense spiral completely out of her grasp.

The look he gave her before walking out was smug and knowing. Insulting and maddening.

She trailed him and, reining in every bit of control she could muster, closed the heavy door behind him. Softly, because she was *not* going to lose control this time.

SAVANNAH KEPT CRAZILY BUSY the next few days, helping Katie with last-minute wedding details. It was a way to avoid Jake and get her hormones under control.

Saturday finally arrived. Wedding day. Insane day. The three Salinger sisters had been running since eight that morning, and for Katie, the eternal night owl, that was quite a feat. Their dad and stepmom had been helping by watching Allie, Logan, Billy and Owen for most of the day, and getting them ready for the ceremony.

"Crap. Only an hour left," Katie said, rushing around in her wedding gown and bare feet.

"You're doing fine," Lindsey said. "Your hair and makeup are done. Gown is on. All you have left is your hose and shoes."

"Do you understand how long it'll take to get panty hose on in this thing?" Katie asked.

"That's what we're here for," Eve, Katie's friend and Noah's receptionist, said. "I got you thigh-highs. Much easier."

"And Noah can remove them with his teeth," Lindsey said. "Pictures don't start for another fifteen minutes. Why don't you sit down and relax while we finish getting beautiful."

"I can't sit in this dress," Katie said, and Savannah laughed.

The door opened and Allie sneaked in, wearing her junior bridesmaid dress that matched the coral of the rest of the others. Each of the dresses had a different style, necessitated by Lindsey's pregnant middle. Savannah's floor-length dress had a halter neckline, and wrapped to the side just under her bodice. Her daughter's had a similar neckline and was full-length, as well. Realizing how grown-up Allie was getting made Savannah's heart swell with a bittersweet mix of pride, sadness and amazement.

"You're gorgeous, honey," she declared.

"Thanks." The single word was said almost shyly, with no venom. After a day filled with stress and arguments, Savannah would accept that happily.

"Everyone decent?" Their dad was at the door, clad in his tux.

"We're dressed," Katie said. "Don't know if all of us would qualify as decent."

He regarded her with a grin on his face. "My little girl. You're beautiful." He went to her and hugged her carefully in order not to crush her dress, or the flower pinned to his lapel.

"Thanks, Daddy." Katie wiped the corner of her eye. "No more. I refuse to cry, so you have to stop the mushy stuff."

Wendell turned to the rest of them. "Wow. All of you. Gorgeous."

"Especially this girl." Katie came over to admire Allie, and Lindsey and Eve joined in. Allie's smile grew. "Nice purse, too. Whatcha got in there?"

"Drawing paper. Pencils."

"Of course," Lindsey said. "Just what every young artist has in her purse."

"You're pretty," Allie told Katie.

"It's the makeup," her aunt said, laughing.

"Can I wear some lipstick?" Allie looked around at them and everyone peered at Savannah.

"Aren't you a bit young?"

"Just this once won't hurt her," their dad said.

Savannah stared at her daughter, wondering when she'd changed from little girl to young lady who asked for makeup. "Anyone have a subtle color?" she inquired.

Lindsey went to her purse for a leather pouch, and dumped out a pile of cosmetics. Sorting through them, she picked up one lipstick and checked the bottom. "Sea coral. This will be perfect."

Their dad went to find his wife, the head babysitter. The four attendants and the bride finished getting ready, then made their way to the sanctuary for Katie's big event.

An hour later, the wedding party and all the guests made their way to the church hall, a building across the parking lot. Thankfully, the facility permitted alcohol. Savannah needed a drink or three before she delivered a toast to the bride. She'd been surprised when Katie had asked her to be maid of honor, but they'd grown a lot closer in the past year. Her sister had been staying at Savannah's when Savannah and Michael had separated, and also when Katie was struggling not to fall in love with Noah. They'd been through a lot together in a few months.

Toast time arrived before Savannah was ready. The best man, Brian from Noah's med school, went first, and kept the crowd laughing. Savannah missed most of his speech because she kept going over what she would say. Then they were all looking at her, waiting for her to join Brian at the microphone. She pulled in a deep breath, got up and took the mic from him.

"To my little sister, the baby of the family. The one who always had to prove she was more daring than the rest of us. She's always been the wild child, so when it seemed she might be falling for this guy—" Savannah pointed at Noah "—we sat back and watched what the crazy single girl would do. And she didn't disappoint. She ran like hell."

Everyone laughed and Savannah drew in another deep breath, trying to get past the lump in her throat.

"We're so excited that Katie met this wonderful man. Now *he* has to live with her, not us." Savannah smiled as everyone laughed again. She motioned to her sister to stand next to her. "All kidding aside, I'm so happy for you, Katie. You've always been our risk taker, but in this you went with the sure thing. You and Noah are perfect for each other. Here's to many, many years of happiness and wild adventures."

Savannah raised her glass and clinked it with Katie's, then the two sisters embraced.

"Thank you," Katie said in her ear.

Savannah nodded. As she opened her eyes, still hugging Katie, she spotted him.

Jake sat at a table across the room, staring at her. The expression on his face was... Hard to say what it was, but he wore a slight grin, and a cross somewhere between smug and...lustful?

"Katie," Savannah whispered. "What is *he* doing here?"

The bride pivoted to see who she was asking about. "Oh." Her smile got too big. "Noah and I wanted him to feel welcome. He doesn't know many people in town anymore...."

"You are so full of it. You think you can set us up, don't you?" Savannah fought to keep the pleasure off her face. God, he looked good.

"Dance with him and I'll leave you alone. Promise," Katie said as she flitted off to talk to more well-wishers.

The deejay was getting ready to begin the dance part of the reception. The kids' table was suddenly empty, so Savannah went in search of her children. In the opposite direction of Jake.

The music started, and the bride and groom shared their first dance as husband and wife. Savannah stopped to watch them. She joined the crowd surrounding the dance floor as Katie danced with their dad and Noah with his mom. Then others joined them, thanks to challenges thrown out by the disc jockey.

Savannah was circling around to the wedding party's empty table when she spotted Logan heading for her.

"Mom, you have to come here," he said, and he grabbed her hand.

"Where are we going?" she asked, bending down to be heard over the music. Her heart beat faster as she wondered what could be wrong.

"You'll find out."

She scanned her son's face and decided he wasn't acting as though something was wrong. Then she figured out where her traitorous child was taking her. Straight to Jake.

Jake, who was damn tempting in a black suit. His shoulders seemed even broader than usual. His hair was as neat as she'd ever seen it, though still a tad tousled on top, and his eyes caught her every move.

"Jake wants to dance with you, Mom."

CHAPTER SEVENTEEN

SAVANNAH GLANCED AT Logan. "You're grounded for life. Now, go find Billy and Owen and your sister, and stay together, in this room."

Logan took off and Jake stood up.

"Coward," Savannah said, having to bend close to him to be heard over the music. Her heart continued to race, but now it was in anticipation instead of fear.

"I like to think of it as strategic." He touched her waist as he spoke into her ear.

The softness of his breath on her jaw and neck sent a shiver through her. She'd hoped avoiding him for the past few days would strengthen her resistance. Apparently, it hadn't.

"Will you dance with me?" he invited. "They're playing our song."

"We don't have a song."

"I know. That was a line," he said, grinning.

She couldn't resist. Not when he looked like *that* and smelled like that and focused all that male attention on *her.*

Savannah accepted his proffered hand, and couldn't help noticing anew how warm and strong it was, how gentle his grasp. She followed him to the dance floor, determined not to let anyone detect how vulnerable she was to this man.

He stopped and faced her, still holding her hand, and their eyes met. He didn't bother to hide the thoughts going through his head—naughty thoughts that involved her and him. Alone.

His hands slipped around her waist and she moved close, so that their bodies touched from chest to thigh. Her dress was cut low in the back and she felt the heat of his hands directly on her skin.

The way she fell into him, closed her eyes and rested her head on his shoulder, soaking in his familiar scent, was almost involuntary.

Realizing how she must appear to everyone around them, hanging on Jake, she straightened a little and glanced up at him.

"You're the sexiest woman here, Savannah."

"Sweet-talking me won't help your case, Jake. Still not marrying you."

He chuckled.

"In fact, consider this a good-bye dance," she said. "After this, we just share a construction project."

"And a child," he said softly.

She avoided his gaze, focusing on everyone else, trying not to think about how right it seemed to be in his arms.

She felt someone watching them from one of the tables. Michael. She'd almost forgotten he was here. Ignoring him, she eased away from Jake as the music faded.

"Do you mind if I ask Allie to dance?" he said before she could escape.

Habitual fear made her chest tighten momentarily. She

followed his line of sight to their daughter, who was laughing with her cousins. Jake wouldn't tell her the truth while they danced, she reminded herself. Allie would love being led around the dance floor by him.

"Just make sure you keep the secret to yourself."

He nodded, one corner of his mouth crooked up smugly.

While Allie was occupied and Logan was busy with Owen and Billy, making fun of his sister from the edge of the dance floor, Savannah escaped the noisy room for a few minutes.

Once she was away from the music, she could hear how her ears were ringing. She kept walking to the outside doors, hoping to cool off and get some fresh air. Her heart still hadn't returned to its normal rate.

Outside, she wrapped her arms around herself and walked a few feet down the side of the building. She leaned against the brick wall, inhaling the brisk, November air, struggling to regain her balance. After about two minutes, the door opened. Michael walked out and stood there, regarding her. Something intangible told her he wouldn't utter a friendly hello.

"I thought you told me nothing was going on between you and Barnes," he began without preamble.

Savannah exhaled tiredly. So much for fresh air and getting away. "Nothing is going on, Michael."

"Looked like quite a bit was between you when you danced."

"We have a history. That's all it is."

Michael chewed on the inside of his cheek as he decided whether he could believe her or not. She straightened, and was about to go back inside when he spoke again.

"He's dancing with our daughter, Savannah."

"He asked me if it was okay."

"Why don't I get a say in that?" Michael asked.

"I didn't feel it was anything to make a federal case out of. Jake cares about her and isn't going to hurt her."

"Oh, so now you're starting to trust him?" Michael's voice rose.

"Calm down," she told him.

"I'm not going to calm down, Savannah. I'm suddenly the outsider and I don't like it. So help me God, if that man breathes a word to her about being her father, I will make him wish he'd never come back to town."

"She's going to find out who he is eventually. You might as well start accepting that. It's no longer just you and me who know the truth."

"That was never part of the deal."

"In case you haven't noticed, the deal changed when we split up. I'm going back inside."

As she walked past him, she realized Michael was right about one thing. She was starting to trust Jake.

CHAPTER EIGHTEEN

"I'M HOLDING YOU UP." Jake's grandma took another dainty bite of her frosted cinnamon roll as she sat next to Jake at the bakery.

"No rush, Grandma. I'm not in a hurry," Jake said. He'd already downed a chocolate-frosted long john and a bear claw and was now finishing his coffee.

He was probably exhausting his grandmother with all the outings the past couple of days, but he was leaving on Monday and wanted her to get out of the house plenty now.

"I'm so glad you stayed an extra week. It's been wonderful having you around."

"My pleasure. I'll miss you and Em when I go back."

A surprise snowstorm had hit his part of Montana last weekend, and very little work was going on at the Clayton job site. His meeting with the movie producer wasn't until next Wednesday, so he'd decided to stick around Lone Oak to attend some additional planning meetings with his grandma and Zach, and to spend more time with his own family. He and Emily had put in hours together, sorting through their dad's house. The only ones he hadn't seen enough of were Savannah and her kids. And his dad. He'd been putting off that final visit.

"Please tell me you won't stay away so long," Odessa said between bites.

"I won't. I'll be back much more often." What with the building project, which he was getting really involved in despite himself, and his daughter, there'd be no keeping him away for long. He'd already decided he'd fly back for the holidays.

Activity right outside the window caught Jake's eye. His pulse sped up when he recognized Savannah, Allie and Logan skipping toward the front door. Even Allie was smiling. They all stopped and laughed at something Logan said, and Jake found himself smiling, too.

"What is it?" his grandma asked. She craned her neck to find out what had caught his attention.

Jake glanced around to discern if anyone could hear him. The other two tables of customers were involved in their own loud conversations.

"That's Allie out there. And her mother and brother." He'd told his grandma all about her great-granddaughter this week. He couldn't wait for the day when the two could meet and acknowledge their relation.

The trio entered the bakery but didn't notice Jake and his grandma sitting on the opposite side by the wall. They were still laughing and carrying on and having fun just ordering doughnuts.

As Jake watched the threesome, something happened inside him. He realized nothing made him happier than those three. Not just Allie; Logan and Savannah, too. He'd fallen hard for the kids early on. As he watched Savannah now, her hands resting protectively on each of her children as they ordered, he knew at once that he loved her.

He hadn't had many chances to see her so relaxed with the kids. Obviously, she was a wonderful mom to them. The best mom they could have.

He'd held a grudge against her for not telling him about Allie earlier, true. But that was gone now. All he could feel was gratitude that she was so good to their child. Admiration, respect…and, yes, love. That was what he felt. God, he loved her.

"She's precious, Jake."

"Yeah. She is. I want to marry her."

His grandma stared at him. "I was talking about the girl."

Jake laughed. "That, too. Sorry. I was lost in my thoughts. I'm going to go talk to them. Remember, Allie doesn't know who I am yet."

His grandma nodded and turned back to her cinnamon roll.

"Hey," Jake said as he came up behind Savannah. The kids were down a ways, crawling up on spinning stools at the counter.

"Hi. What are you doing here?"

"Doughnuts with Grandma. I thought it was Michael's weekend with the kids."

"It is, but he had a business trip and isn't getting back until today. They're going over this afternoon."

"Perfect. Would you like to have dinner?"

She gave the short old man behind the counter a ten, seeming flustered by Jake's question.

"I can't, actually," she said once she'd gotten her change.

"Do you have a date?" The question was supposed to be in jest, but the thought made him edgy.

"I've told you repeatedly I don't date." She opened her wallet to put away the change. "I have to go to my dad's." Her brow furrowed and she acted nervous.

"Have to? Is it dinner?"

Savannah checked on the kids, then faced him. "I have to tell him. About you. Us."

"Ahh. Will it cause problems?"

"I don't know. But I'm dreading it."

"I'd like to come with you, Savannah."

Her head shot back in surprise and, if he wasn't mistaken, suspicion. "Why would you want to do that?"

"I wasn't able to be there for you eleven years ago or anytime since." He shrugged, trying to make light of his offer, because if she knew how much he wanted to go, she'd turn him down. "I'd like to be now."

She considered his words, still not convinced. "It won't be fun. I have no idea how he'll react, but it won't be the typical telling-Dad-we're-expecting scene."

Jake attempted to stifle a grin. "I realize that. I'm not saying you can't handle this alone. There's no doubt in my mind you'll be fine by yourself, as you always are. It's just…I missed out on everything, Savannah. Good and bad. I want to be involved."

"This doesn't mean we're telling anyone else." She glanced pointedly at Allie.

"We can argue about that a different night. Right now, all I want to do is go with you to talk to your dad."

Savannah finally nodded wearily. "Okay. Fine."

"Really? No she-woman stuff?"

"Not right now. Maybe later," she said, almost grinning. "I'll pick you up at six and we can go get it over with."

"HOLY TOLEDO, SAVANNAH. You're just telling me *now?*" Wendell Salinger leaned back on the new mocha leather sofa in the living room of the house he and Claudia had moved into last year. His wrinkled face showed every one of his years—and maybe some extra ones tonight.

Savannah stole a glance at his wife, who removed her glasses to gawk back in disbelief. Her stepmother appeared to be even more shocked than he was. Darn. Usually, Claudia helped her dad come around to his daughters' ways of thinking. He was bowled over by the confession, but she seemed absolutely flattened.

Jake, who sat next to Savannah on the love seat, wrapped his hand around hers and squeezed. Thank God he'd accompanied her. Though she wouldn't say so to him, having him next to her, at her side, was reassuring. An accomplice of sorts. Not that her dad had said anything bad…yet. He hadn't said much at all. She checked to make sure she hadn't sent him into cardiac arrest.

"So you were involved with my daughter back then?" Wendell inquired of Jake.

"Yes, sir." Jake appeared much more relaxed than she felt. He glanced at her, one corner of his mouth curving up. "Then and now."

Savannah's eyes widened. Was he insinuating they were sleeping together again? Because that had been the heart of the matter back then….

"I found out about Allie when I returned to town a few weeks ago. I've been getting to know her ever since."

"Why on earth didn't you tell Jake you were having his baby, Savannah?" her dad asked, sitting forward again.

"In all fairness, I was incommunicado," Jake interjected. "She made an effort to find me, but I didn't want to be found."

Savannah squeezed his hand in gratitude. "Michael helped me. We spent several weeks searching for Jake."

"When do you plan to tell Allie?" her dad asked.

"Soon," Jake said.

"Later," Savannah insisted.

"Do your sisters know?" Wendell asked.

"They do now. They didn't back then," Savannah said. "I'm sorry I didn't tell you, Dad. It's just that…"

"It's okay, Savannah. I'm not sure how helpful I would've been. I still wasn't handling things very well then."

She nodded, aware now he continued to feel guilty for all the time he'd spent in a fog of grief over losing his wife. It'd taken him years to start living again, and Claudia was a big part of that.

Savannah focused on her stepmom again, and her dad followed her gaze.

"You okay, honey?" he inquired.

Claudia nodded and put her glasses back on. "Surprised is all. You've hidden it for a long time."

"I'm sorry," Savannah said. "Not that I didn't trust you guys. Just that I had to make things work with Michael. I had to protect Allie."

"Interesting you say that," her dad said. "I like Michael. Accepted him as a son-in-law and all. But there was something about him… I never did feel he was the right man for you."

Savannah rolled her eyes. "There isn't a right one for me, Dad."

"I don't know about that," he said. "This one here doesn't seem so bad." The two men exchanged a smile, and Savannah wanted to yank Jake out of there before they got too cozy.

"Pardon me for prying, but *are* you two involved again?" Claudia asked, reaching for her husband's hand.

"No." Savannah didn't hesitate for a second.

"I'm trying to convince her to marry me," Jake countered.

She was going to kill him. Slowly.

Both her dad and stepmom turned their full attention to her, as if she needed to justify herself.

"What?" she asked. "I'm not getting married to anyone. Tried it. It didn't work out. End of discussion."

"Michael wasn't your type. Your dad just said so," Jake stated. "Of course it didn't work with him."

"We are not having this conversation here, now or ever." She stood.

"She's a tough nut to crack," Wendell told Jake.

"Dad! Whose side are you on?"

"I want what's best for you, honey. You and Allie, and Logan, too."

"We're doing great, Dad. This is the twenty-first century. Women don't have to be married to have a happy life."

"Can I ask you something, Jake?" Claudia's voice was quiet compared with the two Salingers. "Are you wanting to marry Savannah to be in Allie's life?"

"Claudia…" Wendell's tone was scolding.

"No, it's okay," Jake said. "Fair enough question. I can't wait to be more a part of Allie's life. She's an amazing girl.

But…" He stared at Savannah now, though she avoided eye contact. "I want to marry Savannah because I love her."

She froze and closed her eyes. He'd said that *here?* In front of her *dad?*

A soft, almost dreamy sigh issued from Claudia, which made Savannah's eyes pop open. "We have to go," she announced, and reached for her purse on the coffee table.

Wendell stood then and walked toward her. He wrapped his arms around her and she automatically did the same.

"I love you, honey." He stepped back. "Thank you for telling us. We're here for you. Whatever you need us to do. If that means babysitting so you and Jake can go out and get reacquainted…"

Savannah glared down at Jake and her dad chuckled.

"Appears to me you're getting under her skin, Jake. In my book, that's a move in the right direction."

Jake stood and shook Wendell's hand. "Thank you, sir. She's a stubborn woman."

"I can tell you know her well."

Claudia joined them, putting her hand on Savannah's arm. "Just don't go eloping on us, please, kids. Doesn't have to be a big ceremony, but I'd like to be invited."

Savannah pressed a quick kiss to Claudia's cheek, then pivoted to leave, pulling Jake with her and muttering, "I can't believe this."

"THAT DIDN'T GO SO BADLY," Jake said as he backed her van out of her dad's driveway. Why she'd let him drive over here from his grandmother's house she still wasn't sure. He refused to give the keys up now. He'd gotten in the driver's side and started the engine. Savannah had no doubt he would leave her there just to be ornery, so she'd climbed in the passenger side.

She didn't respond to his assessment. Barely even heard it because the blood was rushing through her head so loudly. Her heart raced and her jaw locked.

Instead of driving to his grandmother's house, he went directly to hers, and that didn't help her temper any.

Once the van had stopped in the garage, she bailed out and hurried up the front steps to the door. Jake caught up with her as she fought with the stupid, antiquated, stubborn lock.

"You think they didn't take it well?" he asked.

Finally, the key twisted and she headed inside. She would've slammed the door in his face had he given her the chance, but he was too close behind her.

Jake had the nerve to remove his jacket and toss it on the chair in the corner.

"I didn't invite you in," she said evenly, in a tightly restrained voice.

"I'm used to it." He followed her into the bedroom, where she set her purse on the dresser. "You're pissed that I told them I wanted to marry you."

"You think?"

He blocked her way out of the room, and instead of fighting him, she crossed her arms and stared him down.

"What's bugging you even more is that I said I loved you."

"What the hell *was* that?" Savannah demanded.

"The truth."

She fought not to get flustered, fought not to miss a beat, but she couldn't help it. Eighty percent of the fight flowed right out of her. As tough as she wanted to be, as much as she needed to be by herself, declarations of love from this man could apparently bring her to her knees. Because she knew, deep down, he wouldn't lie. Would never say he loved her if he didn't mean it.

He leaned one shoulder against the door frame and caressed her cheek until she met his eyes. "That whole thing about my grudge? I told you I'd get over it. I'm over it. You're an awesome mom, and a hell of a woman. I love you, Savannah. And I think you love me, too."

She was weak. At this moment she knew it, but she ceased to care. The kids were gone for the weekend. The truth was out to most of her family. She was worn out from battling her attraction continuously, and this once, she was going to stop fighting and grab what she wanted.

Savannah stepped toward him and ran her hands up his abdomen to his chest, feeling the strength beneath his shirt. God, he had muscles, and she needed to feel them. See them. Taste every last bit of him.

But first she needed to drive him crazy. As crazy as he made her.

The only illumination in the bedroom was from the dim lamp in the living room. She kept it that way and pulled him farther into the room.

She tugged his shirt out of his jeans and started to unbutton it from the top, unhurriedly, trailing her fingertips along his skin between each button. He watched her without speaking, never losing eye contact. That gaze made her heart race. Aroused a longing deep within her that made her ache.

When all the buttons were unfastened, she dragged the

sleeves down his arms and couldn't help admiring those biceps, the pecs. Some guys softened up as they hit their thirties, but not Jake. He'd been in great shape as a teenager years ago, and he'd only improved. Filled out, broadened in all the right places, hardened. She whisked her tongue over one of his nipples and he sucked in his breath. But he didn't touch her. Maybe he sensed that this was her moment and she was going to play it her way. He seemed just fine with that, if the groan that escaped his throat when she swirled her tongue around his other nipple was any sign.

Savannah explored every ridge and dip of his chest, working her way down to his waist, leisurely, following the sparse hair. She unbuttoned his jeans and drew the zipper down painfully slowly. She glanced up at Jake's face, and the look there heated her blood even more. His eyes were half-closed, his lips parted, his breathing uneven.

Good.

She wanted him begging before she could beg herself.

On her knees now, she untied his shoes with shaky fingers. She removed them and tugged his jeans down his legs, then helped him step out of them. Savannah stood, admiring the fit of the navy-blue boxer briefs, and moving so close she could feel his warm breath on her forehead. She longed to devour those lips that were so near, but held back. Instead, she inched her fingers into the elastic band at his hips and slid the shorts down without touching anything but his outer thighs. He moaned as he became naked in front of her, fully revealed while she remained clothed. Not touching him was absolutely killing her.

He stepped out of his briefs and his gaze bored into hers.

She took in the sight of him, every masculine, solid inch and felt a response deep within her body.

"Now what are you going to do with me?" His voice was ragged, husky, so sexy.

She stood on her toes and placed light kisses on his lips, still without touching the rest of him. "Whatever…I…want."

His arms closed around her and he forced her up against his length, pressing his hardness into her. Jake ran his palms over her back, and settled his mouth on hers, kissing her until she was dizzy. She nearly forgot that this was *her* deal. She was the boss for the next half hour, hour, night, however long necessary to make him crazy and to stop this insane craving inside herself.

She pulled away and shook her head, her lips hinting at a smile. Taking his hand, she led him to the end of the bed and gently pushed him onto it. She stood between his knees and drew her sweater up inch by inch, then over her head. Jake moaned again when he saw the red lace she wore underneath. He reached out and cupped one of her breasts, but she took his wrist.

"No touching. Not yet," she said, hardly recognizing her own voice.

She kicked her shoes off, unbuttoned her jeans and wriggled out of them, revealing more red lace, which met with more approval. She smiled, feeling the power of his desire, knowing she could have just about anything from him right now. Knowing she would give him almost anything.

She prolonged the striptease, her hands shaking even more, her knees threatening to give out. She undid her bra and let it slide down her arms to the floor. Then she hooked her fingers into the strings at her hips and eased them downward. In the dim light, she saw Jake swallow as his eyes followed. She inched out of her panties, and the predatory, barely restrained look he sent her made her shiver. And step forward to touch him at last.

CHAPTER NINETEEN

JAKE'S PATIENCE WITH being passive for Savannah's sake was running mighty low. He'd never been this turned on in his life, and seeing as how he remembered in exquisite detail the only other night he'd shared with her, that was saying a lot.

He lay back on her bed now, completely still except for his heart, which slammed against his chest, and his lungs which fought for oxygen. She slid over him teasingly, hovering just above him, not quite making contact. And he waited. Biding his time.

Savannah finally moved in and kissed him, hard, and Jake would have wept with joy if he hadn't been so swept away by the taste of her, the feel of her lips on his. It was as if they'd never kissed, and yet the kiss was so perfect and familiar.

Her body fit between his legs, her breasts pressed against his chest, and that was just about all Jake could stand of lying there under her. He wrapped his arms around her and with one fast move had her beneath him. Surprisingly, she didn't complain. In fact, she became more frantic for him, grabbing his ass, making sexy little noises in her throat.

He needed every bit of willpower to pull back six inches and break the contact of their mouths.

"One thing," he said, sounding out of breath.

"Don't even say it…."

"I'd like to think we're older and wiser, but…birth control? Apparently, we're pretty fertile together."

"Oh. It's okay. I'm on the pill."

"That'll take care of pregnancy."

"Jake, I haven't had sex for almost two years. I'm clean. You're the only one we need to worry about."

"Same for me," he said, secretly thrilled she'd had no one since her divorce. He kissed her again.

"Same for you what?" she asked, inching to the side.

"I'm clean."

"Has it been two years for you? Is that what you mean?"

He went back to kissing her, hoping to distract her.

"Jake."

"What?"

"Tell me."

He drew away and stared down at her. "Not two years. Not quite one year. But I've had a physical. I'm clean. Now…if my recent history checks out okay, can I get back to what I was doing?"

She pulled his head down and got back to it for him, which worked just fine for Jake. When she somehow rolled back on top and straddled him, it was still fine. More than fine. She eased herself down on him, taking him inside her.

This was the closeness he'd ached for ever since he'd first experienced it. For nearly twelve long years, she'd been in his dreams, and still the reality of her blew his mind—which was nothing compared with what she was doing to the rest of him.

Having her on top gave him the erotic show of a lifetime. Her languid sexy movements were driving him mad. Jake reached up for her breasts and ran his thumbs over her pebbled nipples, played with them, pinched them lightly. Savannah threw her head back and arched even more, moaning his name and a jumble of other words that nearly made him lose it.

Their slow pace became more frantic quickly, until Jake knew that if he didn't hold her back he'd lose control too early. To get her to this point had taken him long enough; he was not going to ruin it for her. Grasping her beautiful backside, he again switched their positions and slowed things down a little. A very little, because no matter who was in control, it was too good between them. Her hips rose to meet him at every thrust. He became oblivious to any intention to send her over the edge first, as the need in him built to a fevered pitch, burning through him, making him lose his mind.

Savannah called out his name and dug her nails into his back, and there was no hope for him any longer. He plunged over right after her, losing awareness of everything except the exquisite woman in his arms and the way she made him feel.

Their hearts pounded in unison and they both gasped for air in the aftermath. When Jake could muster the strength, he rolled to his side, Savannah along with him.

"Holy…"

"Yeah," she said with a lazy, satisfied grin. "We're good at that."

"*Good* doesn't seem like the right word."

"I know, but my brain doesn't have enough oxygen to locate a better one."

She trailed her fingertip over his jaw, down his shoulder and onto his upper arm. There, she stopped at a tattoo, which appeared to be healing.

"Is this new?"

He nodded and moved so she could see it. "You might recognize it."

Savannah flipped on the lamp on the nightstand. He feasted his eyes on her nakedness as she inspected his tattoo.

"It's one of Allie's designs." She traced it tenderly.

"You got it. My sister did the tattooing for me. She was very impressed with it."

"I can't believe you did that." Savannah grinned sentimentally. "You're a total softie."

"No way. Softies don't get tattoos." He pulled her closer and ran his fingers lightly up and down her back, thinking he'd like to stay this way for the rest of the weekend. Or longer.

JAKE OPENED ONE EYE, momentarily confused until he recognized Savannah's bedroom. The sun had risen, though the day must be gloomy and overcast, judging by the dimness of the room.

Savannah was tucked up against him, her naked body partly on top of his, her back toward him. He touched her stomach gently, not wanting to wake her but unable to resist the silky feel of her. He stirred just enough to see over her to the clock on the nightstand. Eight-thirty. Perfect. Still some time to wake her in the most erotic way he could conjure and linger in bed with her.

He inched away, and Savannah's body shifted so she was flat on her back. She made no sign that he'd awakened her yet, but he would change that.

Jake leaned over her and trailed his fingers over her nipple, teasing it and pinching it. He could tell she was aware of his touch, though now pretending to still be asleep. That was okay. Two could play that game. He smiled to himself, anticipating the challenge of arousing Savannah.

He took her nipple into his mouth and circled it with his tongue. Savannah tensed a fraction but still didn't open her eyes. He dragged his tongue from her breast to her navel, giving every inch of her skin close attention. She was very obviously awake, breathing unevenly, but still she kept her eyes closed, as if she could fool him.

His kisses moved lower, then lower still, to the place between her legs that was hot and moist, anticipating his touch. At the first caress of his tongue, her body jolted to life, arching toward him as a needy moan escaped her throat.

"Oh, you're awake," he said innocently, grinning up at her.

Her lids were only half-open. "*Awake* is one word for it," she said breathlessly.

"What's another word?" he asked, after suckling and teasing her body some more.

"About to crawl out of my freaking skin," she gasped, arching again.

"You sound like you're having a hard time breathing," he taunted.

"Can't…imagine…why…" She was tunneling her hands through his hair, trying to pull him closer.

"Maybe you should consult a doctor."

He brought her nearly to the edge with his tongue, then crawled up her body, bestowing kisses and nibbling her skin, until he reached her lips.

"You," she said, wrapping her legs around him, "are such a tease."

"You could send me home." He rubbed his hardness against her and she moaned again.

Savannah took control then, directing his shaft exactly where she wanted it to go, then thrusting her hips against him, making him just as wild and hot as she was. Damn, this woman knew how to work magic.

Holding on longer than Savannah demanded a gargantuan effort. The witch was making him crazy. She met every thrust and gradually drove their tempo to a frenzied rush. They rolled over several times and nearly fell off the bed, kicking blankets out of their way, laughing together. When she finally climaxed and called out his name, he let himself go and fell with her.

They lay quietly, still joined intimately, slowly returning to reality.

"Not a bad way to wake up," she said at last, running her fingers over the stubble on his cheek.

Jake couldn't help smiling in agreement. "I could stand to wake up like that for the rest of my days."

Her fingers stopped moving. She dropped her hand to her side and didn't meet his eyes. There was nothing overt, but the expression on her face told him very clearly she had a problem with what he'd just said. A problem with them having a future together.

He was an idiot for believing her seduction last night had any meaning.

He sat up and swung his feet over the side of the bed to the floor, rubbing his face with his hands. Savannah stood on the opposite side and, from the sound of it, drew on her robe.

"So now you're backing out," he said.

"We shouldn't have slept together."

"I don't know," he said, standing and searching for his underwear. "I think it was inevitable."

Savannah shook her head. "I was weak. I'm sorry if you interpreted it—last night—to mean more."

He stared at her, feeling tired. God, so tired. Defeated. "You're doing this again." There was no question in his voice, because obviously, she was running away from him once more. He yanked on his underwear, then shoved his legs into his jeans, his jaw set. "I would've thought that in all these years you'd have grown up enough to handle the intensity. To handle us. Not pull the same thing as before."

"This isn't the same." She wrapped her white robe more tightly around her and crossed her arms in front of her chest.

"Oh? We sleep together and a few hours later you change your mind. I'm not seeing how it's any different."

"The difference," she began, her voice shaky, "is that before, I was scared and might have even made a mistake. This time?" She inhaled deeply and tilted her chin to gaze up at the ceiling. "I know what I'm doing. I let this happen because I wanted it. Wanted to spend the night with you."

He slipped his shirt on with a grimace, then stepped toward her. The expression on his face must have given his anger away, because she edged back.

"You can't have it both ways, Savannah. I won't play that game with you."

"I'm not playing a game…."

"The hell you aren't. You want me enough to have me spend the night when the kids aren't here, but you're too scared to make a commitment and have me in your life full-time. It doesn't work that way. If you want me, you get all of me. You let me into your life and your kids'."

Savannah walked past him. "Is this an ultimatum, Jake? Your way or the highway?"

She kept her back to him, so she didn't catch his nod.

"Yes." He'd never been so sure about anything in his life. "I can't play around with you whenever the opportunity arises, when the kids are at Michael's for the weekend, and then walk away when it's time for you to return to your real life. You can't ask that of me."

She turned around. "I'm not sure I was asking that."

"Then what?"

She shook her head slowly, shoulders sagging. "I still can't marry you, Jake. Not now, not a year from now. We'll just get hurt in the end."

"*Who* will get hurt?"

"You." She met his gaze, her eyes shining with emotion. "Me." She sat on the edge of the bed. "Allie and Logan, too, eventually."

She hadn't changed a bit, he thought angrily, stifling the urge to punch something. "Let me see if I can figure out your theory, here. We get married. Because you went through one bad marriage that ended in divorce, you and I would most certainly end up divorced, too, thereby hurting everyone in the family. The kids would lose another dad, you'd lose another husband…."

"That," she said, springing up, "is exactly what would

happen if I made the humongous mistake of marrying you."

Jake pressed closer to her, his temper raging. "You have feelings for me, Savannah. I know you do or I wouldn't be here. It *is* just like before. You're afraid of what you feel, so you're running away again."

Clenching her jaw, she shook her head. "You're wrong."

"You don't have feelings for me? You expect me to believe that?"

"I do have feelings for you, Jake. I love you." She spat the words at him as if they were a curse, and he stood there, stunned, for several long, confusing seconds.

"You love me." His voice was much quieter. She'd taken all the force out of his anger with that one little admission. Now his heart pounded with cautious hope.

"I love you," she repeated. "Whether I think that's the best idea or not, I freaking love you. Is that what you want from me?"

Jake's mouth flirted with a grin. Not only did she love him, but she'd *admitted it.* "That's a decent start."

"Well, that's all you get. Because sometimes love isn't enough to make things work."

The hope died with her words and the determined look on her face. She marched off to the kitchen and began viciously scrubbing a dirty pan soaking in the sink. Jake followed her and leaned against the wall, watching her.

"I don't understand you, Savannah. I've known you for almost as long as I've been alive, and after all these years, I just don't get you."

"You're not supposed to," she said. "It doesn't concern you."

"You love me, but say we won't work." He straightened and advanced on her. "Yeah, I'd say it concerns me."

He wrested the pan from her and calmly set it in the sink. Her hands were dripping, but he took both of them in his anyway, and turned her toward him.

"Don't do this," she said.

"Do what?"

"Reason with me."

Jake chuckled. "Excellent advice."

He grabbed the towel hanging on the oven handle and dried their hands. Then he looked hard into her eyes and tried like crazy to get through to her.

"Savannah, we've got something between us, a hell of a something. I know you're scared of having another failed relationship, but what if we could make it work?"

She shook her head and broke eye contact. "I'm not scared. I'm just not up for it." She moved a couple of steps away from him. "I don't want to change the way I am. I'm impossible to live with."

"I'm certain you are," he said, and meant it.

"I control everything."

"You controlled everything with Michael."

"Yes. And I would with you, too. It's the way I am."

"Do you really believe our relationship would be anything like yours and Michael's?"

"It's not about the relationship. It's about me, Jake."

He rested against the cabinets.

"What?" Savannah asked.

"Do you remember when you went on your very first date with Michael? It was the summer after we graduated."

"Of course I remember."

"I told you then that he was all wrong for you. You two would never work."

"Right. You know it all, Jake." She threw her hands up as she spoke.

"That's not my point."

"Could you maybe cut to your point? Because we're not getting anywhere and it's just about time for you to go."

"My point is that Moser is a doormat. He was back in high school, and still is today. He's not like you and me, Savannah."

"And what, exactly, are we?"

"Strong-willed. Controlling, yes. Sure of ourselves, sure of what we want. Willing to fight for it."

"A recipe for disaster."

Reasoning with this woman was impossible.

"Michael left you because you were too controlling."

"I know. I was there."

"You could never control me so much that I'd leave."

She actually laughed. "Is that a challenge? Is that your plan? You're going to lure me into marriage by tempting me to prove you wrong?"

"Would it work?"

She stared at him, flushed and flustered. Sexy. "No. My kids' well-being is on the line here. I won't screw with that."

Jake smacked his hand on the counter. "Dammit, Savannah."

"Maybe I shouldn't have let you come over, but it's not as if I've led you on or made you think we had any future together."

But they could if she wasn't so hung up on her twisted logic. Her hard head was standing in the way of their having a life together.

He stared at her for a moment longer, then had to get out of there before he lost it. And God knew this woman could definitely cause him to lose it several times over.

"What are you doing?" she asked, following him as he steamed out of the kitchen.

"Leaving." At the door, he stopped and glanced back at her. "I'll be in touch with you about Allie. I intend to stay in regular contact with her."

Then he left.

CHAPTER TWENTY

THAT WAS IT. Jake was gone. Out of her life.

It was what she'd wanted. What she'd been fighting for since the day he'd first walked into Heartland Construction. Leaving was the right thing to do, because she'd meant every word she'd said to him.

Then why did it feel as if her heart had turned to a rock and stopped beating as he closed the door behind him?

Yes, she *had* meant every word, including the admission that she loved him. She probably always had.

But she truly believed love wouldn't get them through all the fights that would arise from their knocking heads, from her extreme need to be in charge of everything in her life and her kids'.

On the other hand, what would be wrong with being together whenever the kids were gone? Why couldn't they have something casual they squeezed in among everything else? Something fun. Spontaneous. Obligation-free.

Savannah ran her hands through her messy hair and paced. She knew, of course. A relationship between her and Jake could never be casual. Even if she was the type for halfway, there would always be Allie, always that unfinished business.

She shuffled to the living room couch and absently sat

down. The house was so suffocatingly quiet she wanted to scream to shatter the silence. Her throat throbbed with sadness, but her eyes remained dry. After all, this was her doing. This was how she'd wanted it.

She was not going to break down. She'd gotten her way, as lonely as it was. Time to put on her big-girl panties and deal with it.

The kids would be home in a few hours. She had until then to overcome her mixed emotions, to remind herself repeatedly why Jake's leaving was for the best.

SAVANNAH HAD FULLY intended to tackle cleaning the place before the kids got back, but instead, she'd fallen into a deep sleep on the couch. She woke up just minutes before the knock sounded.

The kids bounced in as she opened the door, and for once, she embraced the commotion.

"Hey, guys, how are you?"

Logan rushed into her arms as he usually did, hugging her and jumping into a play-by-play of the day he'd been away. Savannah only half listened as she eyed Michael. He'd been tense every time she'd seen him lately, ever since Jake had come to town.

"Hi, Allie," Savannah said as her daughter walked past her. Her silence was becoming as normal as Logan's noise. "Go get your bags unpacked, kids. Then we can work on homework before dinner."

The children disappeared and she faced Michael, expecting him to move toward the door. Instead he focused on the easy chair in the corner. Savannah followed his gaze and instantly realized the problem.

"Had company this weekend, did you?" He strolled over to the chair and held up Jake's jacket.

"That's my business." She took the coat from him and placed it over the back of the couch, as if she had nothing to hide. It was too late for hiding.

"When my kids are involved, it's not just your business."

"The kids were with you. What I do when they're gone doesn't concern you."

"I disagree."

She eyed him in disbelief. Who did he think he was?

"You can do whatever you want with any man out there, Savannah…any man but him."

She stepped closer, cracking her knuckle. "You have no say in the matter."

"Jake will do irreparable damage to this family, and you know it."

"He's not doing anything to the family. Have you really become this paranoid, Michael?"

"Don't act like I'm being ridiculous, Savannah. He knows the truth and he'll use it to get past you to Allie. He'll tear her world apart."

"He cares about Allie." That, she knew with every fiber of her being.

"What's happened to you? I thought you were in favor of not telling her the truth."

"Telling me what truth?" Allie said quietly from the bedroom doorway.

Savannah's heart stopped and she thought her legs might give out. She braced herself against the wall and closed her eyes.

"Nothing for you to worry about, honey," Michael said, going to her.

The young girl sidestepped and marched into the living room, and the look of determination and stubbornness on her face struck Savannah like a physical blow. And she knew there would be no more hiding. Not if she ever wanted her daughter to trust her again.

"Allie," she said, straightening her spine and trying to garner some strength. "We have to talk. There are things you should know. But give me a few minutes, because there's one other person who must be in on this conversation."

"You're calling… Savannah, what do you think you're doing?" Michael asked.

"I'm going to get everything out in the open," she replied, forcing herself to sound confident. In truth, she dreaded having Jake here again after the way they'd left things. How ironic that Allie had overheard her and Michael when it would be far easier for Savannah to let Jake catch his plane tomorrow and not have to see him for weeks.

JAKE'S GUT CHURNED as he made his way to Savannah's. The scene ahead of him couldn't be pleasant for anyone, but especially not Savannah. Her voice on the phone had been heavy with bottled-up emotion, and though she hid the fear well, he knew she was scared to death of Allie drifting even further from her. That was the last thing Jake wanted. In fact, if he could find a way to get Allie to treat her mother better, he'd do it.

Still, a nervous anticipation buzzed through his veins,

because at long last the secret would be out. He'd be free to tell the world about his daughter and, if he was fortunate, be a father to her at times. He didn't expect miracles, and guessed that Allie would be mad at him, as well, but hope beat stronger in his chest.

The door opened almost immediately when he knocked. Savannah didn't smile, didn't meet his eyes, just stood aside. Her hair was pulled back loosely and her face was pale. Fear radiated off her and he had to check himself to keep from drawing her near. Had to remind himself she'd chosen to handle the rest of her life without him next to her.

One look at Michael told Jake that this meeting wasn't his idea and he thought telling Allie the truth was a mistake. Jake couldn't disagree more. The sooner they told her, the sooner she and Savannah could work through the new reality and rebuild their relationship. Not that that would be simple. It could take months. Maybe longer.

Savannah brushed past him to the hall. "Kids, come on out. Jake's here."

"Logan doesn't need to be in on this," Michael said, alarmed.

"He should know, too. It's time for everyone to know." Savannah met his eyes with a determined stare, and Jake understood how their marriage had gone wrong. Michael was no match for this woman when she made her mind up about something. Which was usually.

Allie arrived then, appearing like a mini Savannah, her face etched in resolve, but with a hint of trepidation. She was doing her best to be tough, though. Jake had to work hard not to grin. A smile wasn't appropriate, yet he was so damn proud of that little girl.

"Why don't we all sit down," Savannah said stiffly.

They filed around the couch. Allie took the love seat. Savannah and Jake both ended up on the sofa and Logan crawled up into Savannah's lap. She invited Michael to sit, but he shook his head and burned a path in the carpet behind the couch.

"Are you going to tell me the truth now?" Allie asked.

"Tell her what truth?" Logan had no idea what was going on. Heck, he still might not comprehend once they explained everything.

"Honey," Savannah began, addressing Allie. "what you overheard your dad and I arguing about…"

"About lying to me."

Savannah inhaled deeply, quickly. "There is something we haven't told you before because the time wasn't right. You weren't old enough to understand."

Jake tensed as he watched his daughter, unable to fully process the significance of this moment and how it would change everything. His heart was thudding painfully. What if she never accepted him? What if, as soon as she found out the truth, she started hating him?

Savannah squeezed Logan absently, wondering exactly how to get through this conversation without losing it.

"You know that a man and a woman make a baby, right?" she finally said.

Allie rolled her eyes in response. "We're not going to talk about *that,* are we?"

"The people who make a baby are called biological parents. I'm your biological mother." Savannah hesitated.

"Jake…" She put her hand on the cushion between them and felt the warmth of Jake's hand settle over hers. "…is your biological father."

The incessant tick of the wall clock in the dining area was the only sound as Allie took in that information.

"You mean Dad…isn't my dad?" Her bravado was gone and her voice was all little girl as she struggled to make sense of Savannah's words.

"He's…your dad in a lot of senses of the word. He's the dad who raised you."

At last Michael came around the couch to kneel in front of her. "I love you very much, Allie. Always have and always will."

She glared at him and curled up in a ball on the cushion. Michael moved back, helpless and shaken.

"Allie, your mom and I met each other years ago," Jake interjected. "We've known each other all our lives. We cared about one another a lot and went on dates."

"I know about doing it." Allie spat the words out. "You and Mom did it."

"Jake wasn't aware he made me pregnant, and he left town. I couldn't find him, and that's when Daddy—" Savannah pointed to Michael to show *which* daddy she referred to. "He helped me. When we couldn't find Jake, he asked me to marry him."

Allie continued to glare, and Logan sat stock-still.

"What about Logan?" Allie asked.

"I'm his father," Michael said.

Logan nodded once, as if he was reassured. God, he was going to be in therapy before he hit adolescence. Allie, too. What had they done to these children?

Savannah switched to the love seat next to Allie, carrying Logan with her. The last thing she wanted was for him to feel unwanted or unimportant because this was all about his sister.

She reached out to put her arm around her, but Allie ducked under it and moved away.

"You have two dads who love you, Allie. And one mom."

"And a brother," Logan added helpfully.

"I don't want two dads," Allie said. She pierced Savannah with a hateful stare. "I knew you would mess it up!"

Jake knelt in front of Allie now. "Kiddo, I realize this is all hard to understand. We grown-ups have made some mistakes and it's all a little confusing. But I love you."

Allie regarded him, tears beginning to fall. "You only liked me because you're my dad. I thought…"

Her sobs filled the room and Savannah's heart shattered. She moved toward Allie again, and this time her daughter didn't brush her off. She just ignored her as she buckled over, shoulders heaving.

"Allie, I like you because you're an amazing person. You're one heck of an artist, you're sweet and you're fun to talk to. I loved you right away because you're my daughter, but that has nothing to do with why I like you."

"Allie," Savannah said, but the girl made no sign she heard her. "Honey, come here."

Allie leaped off the love seat then. "No! Leave me alone. I don't want to talk to you. Any of you!"

She rushed to the bedroom and slammed the door.

Savannah stood and cracked a knuckle, wanting to

punch something. She'd known this was how Allie would take the news, and she hadn't been able to find a way to soothe her daughter or make things easier for her to understand. Hot tears welled, but she was not going to cry in front of these men.

"You two might as well go now. She won't talk tonight. All we can do is be there for her when she's ready."

"I'll go check on her, Mom," Logan said earnestly. Savannah nodded as he went to their bedroom, love for both of her children choking her up more.

Jake walked over to her. "I can stay for a bit. Make sure she's okay."

Savannah shook her head. "I've got it covered."

He didn't look as though he'd back down soon, and that raised Savannah's ire.

"What about you?" Jake asked.

"What *about* me?"

"This is hard on you."

"Yes, it's hard on me. But that didn't concern you when you were so bent on telling her."

"I didn't do this tonight, Savannah. You can't lay it all on me."

"Go, Jake." She grabbed his arm and directed him toward the door. "You, too, Michael."

"Call me when she wakes up in the morning, please. I'll drive over," her ex said.

"It's going to take a while," Savannah replied. "I'll let you know."

Michael glared at Jake and then left.

"Savannah, I'm sorry this hurts so much," Jake said.

She eyed him, her vision blurring from the damn tears.

He had to get out of there, because she wasn't sure how much longer she could keep the sobs in. She tried to nod once, then just bowed her head instead, hoping to hide how close to losing it she was. She held the door open and silently begged him to leave.

"I'll talk to you tomorrow. I can postpone my flight if necessary," Jake said. He found a scrap of paper on the end table and scribbled his number. "Phone me if you need me before then." He hesitated, then walked out the door.

JAKE MADE HIS WAY DOWN the busy hospital halls after leaving Savannah's. This was an overdue visit, one he'd put off until the very last minute.

His dad was asleep when he walked in. Jake settled into a chair against the wall, prepared to wait as long as it took for him to wake up.

Their previous conversation about Jake's mom and Dean's inability to forgive her had weighed heavily on him. Why his dad had been so unforgiving and distracted for all those years made total sense now. That didn't excuse him, by any means—it just made the matter easier to understand.

Recognizing the similarities between his dad and him had been rough, but they existed. Jake struggled with forgiveness, too. He'd thought about little else lately. The last thing he wanted was to end up like his father—unhappy, mostly alone, full of regrets.

Maybe all this thinking had spurred on his realization of how he felt about Savannah, or maybe he'd just been thick-skulled enough not to recognize he'd loved her for years. But whatever had changed, he felt a weight lifted from his shoulders by letting go of the past and no longer worrying about what he'd missed out on with Allie.

Instead of looking back, Jake was looking forward now. Not quite as enthusiastically as he had been twenty-four hours earlier. He slumped in the chair and closed his eyes, seeing Savannah's face in his mind's eye. He still didn't accept her decision, but he wasn't certain what his next move should be.

"Jacob? That you?" The voice was a mere echo of what it'd been two weeks ago.

He opened his eyes and stood. "Yeah, Dad, it's me."

The old man looked terrible, the worst Jake had seen yet. Emily was right—it wouldn't be long now. His dad blinked repeatedly, as if trying to clear his vision, then lifted a bony hand to wipe his eyes. His arm shook with the effort and Jake felt something inside him sink. This really was the last visit.

He located a box of tissues and handed one to his dad. Then he sat on the edge of the bed and gently helped him wipe his eyes.

"Thank you."

"I didn't wake you, did I?"

Dean attempted to smile. "All I do anymore is sleep. I'm glad you're here."

"Me, too. I have some things to say."

"Oh?"

His dad licked his lips repeatedly, and Jake retrieved the pitcher of water, pouring some into a large hospital mug.

"Let's prop you up." He wasn't sure his dad could hold his head up otherwise. He hit the button to raise the bed, then held a straw so his dad could drink.

"All that stuff you told me about Mom the last time I was in…" He sat on the side of the bed again; there was plenty of room because his father occupied so little space. "It made a lot of sense. Hit home pretty hard, in fact. It seems Barnes men aren't good with forgiveness. I just wanted to let you know…I've struggled with forgiving you."

His dad nodded, the movement slight but unmistakable.

"When you apologized to me, I wasn't ready to let go of my anger, but now I am. It's in the past, Dad."

Dean raised a shaky hand and gripped Jake's weakly. Tears filled the older man's eyes and Jake knew he understood. For the first time in years and years, the air was clearing between them.

"You're a better man than me," his dad said.

Jake studied him and saw he really believed that. "Nah. I just got some good advice."

They sat there, not speaking but feeling more peaceful than they probably ever had together.

"I've got something else to tell you," Jake said after several minutes. He checked to make certain his dad was still awake. Surprisingly, he was. "I have a daughter. An eleven-year-old little girl I never knew about until I returned to town. You're a grandfather, Dad."

His dad's lips moved as if he was trying to speak, but nothing came out.

"Her name is Allie and she's amazing." He told him all about her and his dad paid rapt attention, a rusty chuckle emerging from him every once in a while.

"I wish you could meet her, but she kind of hates me right now."

"Sounds pretty par for the course."

"She found out tonight that I'm her father. It pretty much turned her whole life upside down, but I think we'll be able to work through it."

His dad nodded and they fell silent again for a long while.

"I'm considering moving back to town," Jake finally said, amazing himself, since he hadn't ever put words to the idea. "I want to be in her life, and that won't be easy from twelve hundred miles away."

Dean nodded. "If you move, you could see her every week." His voice was more animated now than when Jake had first arrived, though still very weak.

"My company in Montana is just taking off, though." Jake explained about his two Hollywood clients and how he hoped to build a name for himself with that crowd. He went on for longer than he'd intended, his excitement about his career fueled.

"So you're torn," his dad said when he'd finished.

Jake nodded. "That's one word for it."

"I can give you my opinion, if you'd like."

Jake gestured for him to continue. "Shoot. Please."

"You're trying to choose between your family and your job, in essence. I had the same dilemma, though the circumstances weren't so dramatic. I chose my job." He shook his head sadly. "These past few years have been lonely, but the loneliness really hits home when you lie in a hospital bed for weeks, spending most of your time by yourself. Without family."

Jake's chest ached with sorrow for this man.

"None of that is your doing, son. All mine. I made a

choice, and I feel confident telling you now it was the wrong one."

He fell silent and closed his eyes. Jake didn't move, suddenly afraid that this was it, that his father was going to take his last breath as he sat there on his bed. He covered the old man's hand with his and sighed with relief when those eyes opened again.

"A job won't keep you company on cold nights and holidays," Dean said, and shut his eyes again.

Emotion roiled inside Jake. He sat there for several more minutes, watching his dad, thinking about his words, knowing what he had to do.

Then he stood and bent over his sleeping father. "I have to go."

The old man's eyes opened once more and he struggled to focus on Jake.

"Thanks, Dad. I love you," Jake said in nearly a whisper.

"Love you, too, son."

Jake brushed his hand over his dad's wispy hair, then walked out of the hospital room.

CHAPTER TWENTY-ONE

SAVANNAH WOKE UP before her alarm went off the next morning. Her head throbbed and her mouth was dry, as if she'd gone on one heck of a bender the previous night. She groaned as the evening came back to her.

Heart heavy, she jumped out of bed, grabbed her robe and dragged it on as she made her way across the hall to the kids' room. The door was closed. All was silent and she instinctively knew no one was stirring.

Savannah quietly pushed open the door, needing to reassure herself that everything was okay for now, knowing when Allie got up the day would be one of the most trying of her life.

Logan, whose bed was opposite the door, sprawled diagonally across his twin mattress, blankets twisted at his feet. A sleeping child always brought a certain calmness to Savannah.

She glanced over to Allie, her lips still hinting at a smile—and her heart stopped.

Allie wasn't in her bed. The covers were pulled up semi-neatly, free of child-size lumps. Not breathing, Savannah backed out of the room and did a frantic search through the other rooms of the house, her own included.

Finding no sign of Allie, she raced back to the kids'
bedroom and whipped the closet door open, hoping…

To no avail.

Fear clogged her throat and threatened to choke her. An
inability to accept the worst had her searching through the
house again, this time checking under furniture and in all the
other closets. When she passed the cordless phone in its
cradle, she grabbed it, then held it as she continued her
search.

Her baby girl. Where was her baby girl? God, please let
her be okay.

Staring at the phone, she considered whether dialing
911 was the right thing to do. Her head felt as if it were
full of molasses. Finally, Savannah acknowledged to
herself this really was happening and that it was an emergency. She hit Talk and dialed.

"Nine-one-one, what is your emergency?"

Savannah swallowed hard. "My girl…my little girl is
missing. I think she ran away."

"How old is your daughter, ma'am?"

"Eleven." Savannah was on autopilot.

"Did something upsetting happen?"

Savannah nodded, as if the woman could hear her. She
couldn't speak, couldn't get enough air.

The dispatcher asked her several more questions and
said a car was on its way.

Hanging up to face the too-quiet house triggered the
tears, and her shoulders shook with her wrenching sobs.

Allie had to be okay.

Savannah couldn't handle anything bad happening.
Could not handle it.

Without thought, she hit the talk button again and dialed the number Jake had left for her last night. She told him Allie was missing. He inquired if she'd talked to Michael yet, then said he'd take care of calling him. In less than two minutes, Jake was off the phone and on his way over.

Savannah blindly dug a long-sleeved T-shirt out of her drawer and threw it on, then found sweatpants and socks. Standing in the center of her bedroom, she couldn't seem to think where she kept her shoes. She turned in a slow circle to find them, trying to hold in the sobs. Her old tennis shoes in the corner by the closet door finally registered in her brain, and she stuffed her feet into them.

Without stopping for a jacket, she barreled out the front door to see if, by some chance, Allie hadn't gone far. But no one hid behind the bushes or around the corner of the duplex. There weren't any other places to hide in their yard, and Savannah couldn't go any farther and leave Logan alone.

Helplessly, she went back, still scanning the area as she walked to the front door. Nothing was moving. It was a cold day and no birds or squirrels or rabbits had dared to venture forth to forage.

Where would Allie have gone?

Savannah dialed Lindsey, feeling dumb for not trying her earlier. But her sister hadn't heard from Allie. She promised to drive over right away.

Logan rounded the corner from his bedroom then and Savannah hugged him to her, unable to speak.

"What's wrong, Mom? Where's Allie?"

That made Savannah's breath catch on a sob.

"I'm not sure, sweetie. The police are coming to help us search for her."

"Will they have their sirens on?" he queried somberly.

"I don't think so." Savannah fought down her panic and bent to her son. "Did you hear Allie make any noises in the night?"

Logan considered, then shook his head.

Within minutes, a policeman—Kurt Humphrey, whom Savannah had been a couple of years behind in school— was at the door to get information and start a search.

Savannah wished his presence made her feel better, but it was all she could do to sit and answer his questions, while her daughter was out there…somewhere. Possibly by herself. She refused to entertain any other possibilities because anything else would be even worse.

JAKE AND MICHAEL ARRIVED at Savannah's at the same time. Judging by the cars in the driveway, they weren't the only ones who'd rushed over as soon as they'd heard.

"Thanks for calling me," Michael said as the two men went up the stairs.

Lindsey answered the door as soon as they knocked, and practically yanked them inside. Mr. and Mrs. Salinger sat at the dining room table, worrying. Katie and Noah were on the love seat.

Jake sought out Savannah, who was curled up in the corner easy chair. Her hair was a mess, her eyes looked as though she hadn't slept and the worry etched into her face instantly made her seem five years older.

Instinct propelled him over to her. Ignoring her vibes, which said stay the hell away, he pulled her into his arms. He was shocked when she didn't belt him or push him back. Instead, she buried her face against him and stood there, not crying, not moving. Not putting her arms around him—but that was okay. That she accepted his comfort was enough.

"It's going to be all right," he whispered. "We'll find her, get her home and start helping her cope."

Savannah hesitated, then nodded. He had the feeling she was fighting to keep from crying. He pulled her even tighter and kissed her forehead. Then he released her.

"Let's get busy hunting for her. What's the plan?"

"The police are out searching for her, but…"

"The rest of us will get out there and help," he said. "You stay here in case she returns home."

Savannah nodded again. Jake took charge, splitting up the town between Michael, himself, Noah and Katie and the elder Salingers. Lindsey would stay with Savannah and Logan. Apparently, Zach was already out searching, with the kids in tow.

"I'm going to borrow your van," Jake said. Savannah handed him the keys without blinking. He held up his cell phone. "Call me when you hear something."

She didn't reply, and the terror in her eyes grabbed him. He went back to her and clasped her hands as the others left.

"We'll get through this and everything will be okay. This is the worst part. Just hang in there. Allie's going to need you."

"I doubt she'll let me in."

"Eleven-year-olds get confused sometimes." He gave her a brief smile, the words *I love you* on the tip of his tongue. But he kept them to himself. That was his problem—one he would reckon with later, after they'd found their daughter.

THE NEXT HOUR LASTED an eternity. Savannah paced, cleaned, answered Lindsey when necessary and made promise after promise to God if he'd only let her child return home safely.

"More coffee?" Lindsey asked her, carrying in a full pot.

Savannah picked up her mug from an end table so Lindsey could fill it.

"Sit down," Savannah told her. "Your back has to be aching by now."

"My back is always aching. If I sat down whenever it hurt, I'd never get up." But Lindsey lowered herself to the couch next to where Savannah had collapsed yet again.

"I've never felt so helpless in my life," Savannah said numbly.

"I know. It's horrible just sitting here. But if she happens to come home…"

Savannah stood and opened the front door to the main hallway, then went outside on the front step. She shivered as the wind blew through her thin T-shirt. Seeing no sign of Allie, she went back inside.

She picked up the cordless phone and pressed the talk button, then turned the phone back off. If anyone knew anything, she would've gotten a call. She paced to the kids' bedroom and checked on Logan, who was busy drawing a card for his sister. Lindsey, bless her heart, had convinced Logan that Allie would be home very soon and that she would require some extra love and care for a while.

Savannah just wished she believed that as wholeheartedly as her son did.

The phone rang in her hand, making her jump out of her skin.

"Hello?"

"We've found her," Jake said. "She's okay."

Savannah's entire skeletal system failed her and she slid to the floor in relief. "Where?"

"She went to my grandma's house to see me. Grandma phoned and I'm on my way there. She says Allie's fine, a little cold and scared, but okay. We'll be over as soon as I pick her up. Call Michael and tell him to get to your place, too."

"Oh, thank you, God." Savannah closed her eyes. Allie had walked to Odessa Levine's? "How did she know where your grandma lives?"

"Phone book, apparently. Smart kid."

Savannah nodded, unable to speak as tears rolled down her face. Lindsey moved toward her, her eyes questioning. She nodded and mouthed, "They've found her."

Lindsey carefully sat on the floor next to her and threw her arms around her.

"Savannah?" Jake said. "You still there?"

"Yeah," she squeaked.

"We'll be over in ten minutes." He hung up, and Savannah let out the sobs.

When her crying slowed down, she jumped up and went to the door to wait for them, asking Lindsey to call Michael.

Savannah watched her van whip around the corner a few minutes later and pull into the driveway. She ran down the concrete steps to meet Allie.

Wordlessly, she wrapped her arms around her daughter, and again tears fell. She'd never cried so much in her life, and right now she didn't care.

"Thank God you're all right, Allie," she finally said, after a long look at her. "Let's get you inside and warm you up."

Allie started crying then, too, but she allowed Savannah to hold her hand. When Jake reached them, he lifted Allie, kissed her and carried her inside.

Lindsey opened the door for them. "I've phoned Michael, Dad, Katie, Zach and the police. Everyone will give you guys some privacy now, some breathing room for Allie. I'm going to take Logan with me, let him play with the boys."

Savannah hugged her sister. "Thank you. I've got to go figure out what the heck to do next, after duct-taping Allie to my wrist."

A FEW MINUTES LATER, it was clear all was not well. Allie refused to speak to Savannah or Michael, and only answered questions when Jake asked them.

Allie said she'd wanted to talk to Jake about staying with him, and that was why she'd walked to his grandma's house. He promised that he would have her out for a sleep-over the next time he was back in town. The promise seemed to calm her down a little.

Jake made her swear she wouldn't disappear again, no matter what happened.

"The sleepover's off if you try any funny stuff before then," he told her. "Deal?"

Allie nodded.

"Allie, we all love you very much," Savannah insisted. "I know you probably don't understand everything that's going on...."

"I get it, okay?" Allie said.

"Well, great. Then you're ahead of me," Savannah replied. "This will take awhile for all of us to get used to. But there's one thing you should know. The reason we didn't tell you about Jake earlier is that we didn't want to hurt you."

"You hurt me."

"We knew it would upset you," Michael said. "None of us wanted you to go through this."

Allie crossed her arms. "Can I go to my room now?"

She appeared absolutely exhausted, and Savannah wondered exactly when she'd left the house. "Go rest. Tell everyone goodbye for now. And why don't you write down Jake's cell phone number in your notebook. I bet he would like it if you called him when he's in Montana."

Savannah glanced at Jake and he nodded.

Grudgingly, Allie found her pad of paper for him to write his number on.

Jake hugged her, told her again how much he loved her, then kissed her forehead.

Allie glared at Michael, ignored Savannah and went to her room.

Michael stood. "I guess that's all for now. Let me know what's next. I have to check in at work, but I can come back if you need me."

He walked out the door, leaving Savannah and Jake alone.

"I have to go now, too. I rescheduled my flight for tonight. Call me if there are any Allie emergencies, please."

Savannah didn't want him to leave, but they'd already been down that road. So when he went to the door and said goodbye, she didn't move, just sat there on the couch, wishing she knew where she'd gone so absolutely wrong with everything in her life.

CHAPTER TWENTY-TWO

SAVANNAH DID HER BEST to act as though everything was normal, but obviously, it was anything but.

She'd put fish sticks and Tater Tots on the table half an hour ago. Logan, who'd chattered nonstop since Lindsey had dropped him off, had eaten more than his share. Savannah herself had picked at a few of each. Allie had reported to the table when Savannah had forced the issue, had even put two fish sticks on her plate, but she had yet to have a bite of anything. And if Savannah knew her stubborn child at all, she wouldn't eat a thing.

Which of course worried Savannah like crazy. Throughout the day, she'd tried gentle urging, reasoning, then all-out ordering, to get Allie to eat, but the girl had refused.

Savannah knew when she couldn't win, and this was one of those times. Allie was hurting badly and needed to lash out. No matter how often Savannah reminded her she was only hurting herself by not eating, her daughter ignored her. So…Savannah decided to let her daughter get really good and hungry if she so chose.

But she wasn't going to sit there and watch.

"Logan, you may be excused whenever you're finished

eating. Then you can play quietly in your room for a while. I'll be outside getting some air."

Allie met her gaze with one of anger. Savannah didn't return the sentiment, though. All she felt was a deep sorrow that she couldn't help her child. That and utter helplessness.

After grabbing her jacket, she went out to the front and sat on the top step. The bulb had burned out, and there were no streetlights close, which suited her perfectly.

She leaned her elbows on her knees and bent over, out of tears and out of ideas to aid her daughter or herself.

She'd made a royal mess out of the situation. Not just today or this week or this month. She'd been trying so hard to control things, from her children to her emotions to every little aspect of her life, that everything had gotten screwed up.

So much for trying to control her daughter. Allie had found a way around that by refusing to eat. She hadn't had a thing to eat, the one thing Savannah couldn't force. The joke was on her.

And controlling her own emotions? God. She was a basket case. Not just about Allie. Look how well she'd stood up to her feelings for Jake.

What she wouldn't give to have him here now.

She raised her head from where she'd buried it in her arms. Had she really just thought that? He was gone, as he was supposed to be. Sure, she'd hear from him regarding Allie, but that was it.

She didn't begrudge him time with Allie. Now that the truth was out, she was as willing to have her be with Jake as with Michael. No, visitation wasn't the problem. The problem was that Jake would be no more than her daughter's father, someone who would call her or pick her up to visit him whenever he was in town. When Michael collected the kids for the weekend, she felt no emotion for him. He was merely a fact of their lives. But she knew she would never feel so indifferent toward Jake, not in a dozen years or more.

There again, her need for control was messing things up. If she could just get over her fear... Yes, she was scared. Control and fear of losing had been wrapped up together for her ever since her mom had died. Her mother's sudden death, caused by a drunk driver, had affected Savannah profoundly. The loss had been so great that she'd made up her mind then, even at age fourteen, barely a teenager, that she would never leave herself vulnerable to loss again. She had run from strong feelings ever since.

It was true, though she'd never really realized it before now.

She stood and walked slowly, absently, down the steps.

With her sisters, she'd always put up barriers. Did what she could to keep them from knowing her too well, and vice versa. Only in the past couple of years had she and Katie gotten better acquainted, and then just because they'd both gone through tough times.

Years ago, Michael had felt like a haven compared with Jake. She laughed humorlessly. He'd been safe because she'd never been in love with him. He'd never made her feel she was falling helplessly without a net to catch her. Nothing like Jake, who could merely look at her and make her feel to her very soul.

Her kids—well, she'd fallen in love with them the day

they were born, probably even before. They were her Achilles' heel, she imagined. She'd spent all these years trying to control things in order to protect them from any pain.

And here they were. In a world of hurt and confusion.

Savannah jammed her hands into her jacket pockets and strolled around the double-wide driveway, shaking her head and at the same time feeling a spark of hope.

Obviously, clinging to control so desperately was getting her nowhere except crazy. Control had helped to distance her daughter from her, and had cost her the man she loved.

Could she learn to lighten up? Be less frantic about having everything go as she wanted it to?

She'd open herself up to a whole new brand of hurt, without a doubt. But right now, her heart was in so much pain she didn't see how it could hurt worse. In fact, the more she considered having Jake in her life permanently, every day, at her side, the more she felt her life could be a whole lot better.

She rested against the closed garage door and thought about him. Remembered how it had felt when, amid all her fear and worry about Allie, he'd pulled her close. He hadn't been able to fix things, but his touch had made them…not quite as bad. Being held by him had centered her, calmed her somewhat.

She realized now that he'd taken control. And she'd needed him to do that. Suddenly, what he'd been trying to get her to see about the two of them made sense. As he had said, she could never control him so much that he'd leave, because he wouldn't allow her that power. He was nothing like Michael, and that would make all the difference in the world between them.

She could lean on him when she needed to—something she'd never been able to do with her ex-husband. When she'd been alone, pregnant and terrified, yes, Michael had been there for her, but in a passive way. He'd never once taken control. She likely hadn't wanted him to.

She shook her head. There was no sense wasting any more time out here. She knew what she had to do.

"WHY ARE YOU LETTING ME stay up late?" Allie asked suspiciously, as Savannah tiptoed out of the kids' room.

"We have some girl stuff to talk about."

Allie groaned. "I'd rather go to bed."

"Not that kind of girl stuff. I have things to tell you, discuss with you. Come on." She held her hand out, and when Allie still hesitated, Savannah said, "You're not in trouble. I am."

That got her daughter's attention. They went to the couch and stretched out on opposite ends.

"I've made a bunch of mistakes, Allie. For years and years."

Her daughter sat up and stared at her, speechless.

Savannah told her about how her mother had been killed when she was just three years older than Allie, how awful that had been and how much it had hurt her. She tried to explain how she'd felt—that she never wanted to experience pain like that again.

"I knew it hurt so badly because I loved her so much."

Tears glistened in Allie's eyes.

"And that's when I decided that loving people was too painful."

Her daughter frowned. "You always say you love me and Logan."

"I love you two more than you'll ever know. Maybe when you have your own kids you'll find out. I couldn't fight that if I wanted to. But everyone else... I've tried really hard not to care so much."

"That doesn't sound very smart," Allie said.

"Why is that so easy for an eleven-year-old to figure out, but so hard for a thirty-one-year-old?" She sat up in the middle of the couch to make eye contact with Allie. "I've decided that was dumb and that it might be better to do things differently. And I'd like to tell you my plans."

Allie looked confused but interested.

"The man I love, the one I've probably always loved?"

Allie sat up straighter. "It's Jake. I know it is."

"You are so smart." Savannah reached out and hugged her. "I was thinking that if I'm going to start being smarter and not scared of caring, I should probably see if Jake will marry me. What would you think about that?"

"What would happen to Daddy?"

"Daddy will be in your lives as much as you want him to be. Living with Jake might mean moving to Montana, but we'd make sure that was all right with your dad first. And if it's okay, you could e-mail Daddy, call him, visit him. Could you live in Montana? They have lots of horses there."

Allie pondered awhile. "Maybe. If there're horses, and you and Jake and Logan are there."

"That's my girl."

"And you won't make Jake go away?"

"I hope he'll never ever go away. So I'm going to go for it."

Allie nodded very seriously. "I hope he'll never go away, either, Mom."

That her daughter still wasn't smiling didn't escape Savannah. The happiness would come eventually, she hoped.

CHAPTER TWENTY-THREE

SAVANNAH LEANED BACK in the driver's seat of the rental car and closed her eyes for a moment.

She was really doing this.

Opening her eyes, she reassured herself that the directions were on the passenger seat beside her, her cell phone was in the center console and the heat was blasting full force.

The Butte airport was nearly deserted when she'd arrived after 9:00 p.m. The weather was cold, and she crossed her fingers before taking the car out of park. Not a good night to get lost.

Jake had no idea she was on her way. Her entire family had united behind her when she'd approached them with her idea, bringing her to tears. Lindsey and Zach had invited Allie and Logan to stay with them, and her dad had volunteered to pay for her plane ticket. She'd promised to reimburse him when she could, but he'd waved away the idea, hugged her and wished her luck. Katie had cheered her on and thrown in a couple "I told you so's." Just thinking about them all and their undying support brought fresh tears. She wiped her coat sleeve across her eyes and decided to get on with her mission. They'd all be pissed if she sat here and froze to death in the airport parking lot.

The roads in Montana sucked. She followed a highway for a few miles, but the directions called for her to turn off onto a frighteningly narrow gravel road. About five or six gravel roads later, Savannah had no earthly clue where she was. There was no light to speak of, except for her dome light, and it was barely bright enough to read the map.

This was crazy. She had no idea what to expect when she found Jake. Maybe he'd changed his mind about getting married, especially after he'd gotten a flavor of the Salinger children's drama. Or maybe she'd convinced him she was too controlling, and he would send her away.

She hoped for his sake he hadn't, because she would *not* accept no for an answer. Not after switching flights twice and riding that dinky little plane all the way from Salt Lake City. Not after having her dad pay the equivalent of two weeks' of her wages to get her here. Not after she'd told Allie she would do everything in her power to keep Jake around.

She'd been on this road for too long. She pulled off to the side—not that there was any other traffic, anyway—and consulted the map again. Dammit, she was no longer certain where she was or where she was supposed to be. The more she studied the map, though, the more she thought she was still on track. The drive to the ranch just wasn't supposed to take this long.

Refolding the map, she drew in a deep breath. "Almost there. Have to be close now," she told herself.

Before starting up again, she peered in every direction, hoping to see the lights of a house or a barn. Even if it wasn't Jake's, at least she'd know she wasn't all alone out here. She felt like the only human for miles and miles.

But half an hour later, she became convinced she'd made a wrong turn or missed one. Panic began creeping in as she imagined running out of gas and freezing by the side of the road. So close to finding the man of her dreams, but...

She shook her head and admonished herself that she was losing it. Then she spotted the cell phone and reached for it. She would ruin the surprise by calling Jake and asking for help, but at least she'd show up alive.

She waited for a signal. Nothing. No bars. She swore a long stream of the most colorful words she could come up with, and decided to drive farther to see if she could pick up a signal. Finally, about a mile and a half down the road, she got one blip on the signal bar. She hit the brakes and stopped right in the middle of the road.

Her fingers shook as she pressed the numbers to Jake's cell, but when she was almost finished dialing, it hit her that he probably didn't have a signal, either. She held the phone to her ear, crossing her fingers.

He answered after two rings, and it was all she could do not to whoop and holler and scare the crap out of him.

"Hello?" he said again.

"Jake, where *are* you?" she asked, tears blurring her vision.

"I'm in Montana. Savannah, what's wrong?"

"Where in Montana are you?"

"At my house."

"Where in the name of God is your house in Montana, because I've been driving around for two hours now, trying to find it, and if I don't reach it soon, I'll be eaten by bears or wolves."

"Savannah…" He laughed happily. "Wolves don't eat people, but you should probably be worried about bears. What in the world are you doing here?"

She made a frustrated sound. "Surprising you."

"Where are you exactly?"

"If I knew, I wouldn't be lost." She told him where she'd last known she was.

"That road isn't far from me at all. Any idea where on it you are?"

"No, Jake."

"Stay put. Don't move, and don't open the door to any bears. I'll be there soon."

Savannah disconnected and began laughing hysterically. Instead of grandly surprising Jake, she had to be rescued by him.

In less than ten minutes, a vehicle approached from behind her and slowly drove past. She couldn't see the interior of the dark-colored truck, but the vehicle pulled over in front of her and stopped. She waited, a billion different emotions swirling within her, until Jake climbed out of the driver's side.

Savannah was out the door, racing to him, as soon as she recognized him. She ran right into him and threw her arms around him. He embraced her for several seconds, then gazed into her tear-filled eyes.

"Wow. You're really happy I'm here," he said.

"I'm scared of bears," she said through her laughter. She tugged him to her again, unable to get enough of him, the outdoorsy scent of him, the roughness of his stubble on her cheeks, the feel of his arms wrapped around her.

She breathed him in and attempted to get control of

herself. Then she laughed again, remembering her vow not
to worry so much about control.

"Marry me, Jake. Please?"

The smile that came over his face was worth every
single obstacle she'd encountered that day, from the
layovers and transfers, to the toy plane, to the endless
gravel roads. Her heart felt as if it would explode with the
power of his smile.

Then he shook his head and her heart sank.

"That won't work, honey."

Savannah froze. "What do you mean?"

"You can't ask me to marry you. I asked you first. It's
my proposal."

Her eyes fluttered shut and she almost collapsed with
relief. But she straightened, recovering quickly. "You may
recall," she said, struggling not to smile, "that I rejected
you. Several times."

He lifted her and carried her to his truck. "Ah, yes, how
could I forget? You've kept me guessing about when that
thick skull of yours would allow you to see the light."

"Put me down for a second," she said, and he set her on
the uneven gravel. "You gave me this whole song and
dance about the two of us having a partnership, being
equal, sharing control, blah, blah, blah. So why don't we
just agree that getting engaged is the thing to do."

Jake stared at her, looking very serious, then a grin
crept back across his face. "That sounds like an excellent
idea."

"The kids and I can move here as long as you give us a
few weeks to prepare…."

His grin got bigger. "Actually, that won't be necessary.

I put my house on the market yesterday. I'd decided to move to Lone Oak with or without your blessing. I want to be with my family. My grandma, my sister, my daughter."

"What about your company? Your dream?"

"I'm making my right-hand man a partner. He'll run it. I trust him. The company will be here if we ever want to return. You and the kids have become more important to me."

She wrapped her arms around him. "If you're sure, Jake, then that's okay with me."

"I'm sure. And you know what's even better?"

"What?"

"A very short engagement."

"We have to have a ceremony or Claudia will disown me."

He paused, considering it. "All right," he said, "I'll make you a deal. We'll let Claudia have her ceremony… if you come to my house and start pretending you're my wife right now."

Savannah laughed. "Seems like a tempting deal."

"It can be our little secret," he said, setting her inside his truck.

"What about my car? My bag is in it."

"What's in your bag?"

"My clothes…"

"Honey, where we're going, you won't have any need for those."

She laughed and moved over enough for him to climb in and start them off on the rest of their lives together.

* * * * *

*Celebrate 60 years of pure reading pleasure with
Harlequin® Books!*

*Harlequin Romance® is celebrating by showering you
with* DIAMOND BRIDES *in February 2009.
Six stories that promise to bring a touch of sparkle to
your life, with diamond proposals and dazzling
weddings, sparkling brides and gorgeous grooms!*

Enjoy a sneak peek at Caroline Anderson's
TWO LITTLE MIRACLES,
available February 2009 from Harlequin Romance®.

"I'VE FOUND HER."

Max froze.

It was what he'd been waiting for since June, but now—now he was almost afraid to voice the question. His heart stalling, he leaned slowly back in his chair and scoured the investigator's face for clues. "Where?" he asked, and his voice sounded rough and unused, like a rusty hinge.

"In Suffolk. She's living in a cottage."

Living. His heart crashed back to life, and he sucked in a long, slow breath. All these months he'd feared—

"Is she well?"

"Yes, she's well."

He had to force himself to ask the next question. "Alone?"

The man paused. "No. The cottage belongs to a man called John Blake. He's working away at the moment, but he comes and goes."

God. He felt sick. So sick he hardly registered the next few words, but then gradually they sank in. "She's got *what?*"

"Babies. Twin girls. They're eight months old."

"Eight—?" he echoed under his breath. "They must be his."

He was thinking out loud, but the P.I. heard and corrected him.

"Apparently not. I gather they're hers. She's been there since mid-January last year, and they were born during the summer—June, the woman in the post office thought. She was more than helpful. I think there's been a certain amount of speculation about their relationship."

He'd just bet there had. God, he was going to kill her. Or Blake. Maybe both of them.

"Of course, looking at the dates, she was presumably pregnant when she left you, so they could be yours, or she could have been having an affair with this Blake character before..."

He glared at the unfortunate P.I. "Just stick to your job. I can do the math," he snapped, swallowing the unpalatable possibility that she'd been unfaithful to him before she'd left. "Where is she? I want the address."

"It's all in here," the man said, sliding a large envelope across the desk to him. "With my invoice."

"I'll get it seen to. Thank you."

"If there's anything else you need, Mr. Gallagher, any further information—"

"I'll be in touch."

"The woman in the post office told me Blake was away at the moment, if that helps," he added quietly, and opened the door.

Max stared down at the envelope, hardly daring to open it, but when the door clicked softly shut behind the P.I., he eased up the flap, tipped it and felt his breath jam in his throat as the photos spilled out over the desk.

Oh, lord, she looked gorgeous. Different, though. It

took him a moment to recognize her, because she'd grown her hair, and it was tied back in a ponytail, making her look younger and somehow freer. The blond highlights were gone, and it was back to its natural soft golden-brown, with a little curl in the end of the ponytail that he wanted to thread his finger through and tug, just gently, to draw her back to him.

Crazy. She'd put on a little weight, but it suited her. She looked well and happy and beautiful, but oddly, considering how desperate he'd been for news of her for the past year—one year, three weeks and two days, to be exact—it wasn't only Julia who held his attention after the initial shock. It was the babies sitting side by side in a supermarket trolley. Two identical and absolutely beautiful little girls.

* * * * *

When Max Gallagher hires a P.I. to find his estranged wife, Julia, he discovers she's not alone—she has twin baby girls, and they might be his. Now workaholic Max has just two weeks to prove that he can be a wonderful husband and father to the family he wants to treasure.

Look for TWO LITTLE MIRACLES
by Caroline Anderson,
available February 2009 from Harlequin Romance®.

CELEBRATE
60 YEARS
OF PURE READING PLEASURE
WITH HARLEQUIN®!

We'll be spotlighting a different series
every month throughout 2009
to celebrate our 60th anniversary.

Look for Harlequin® Romance in February!

**Harlequin® Romance is celebrating by showering
you with Diamond Brides in February 2009.**

Six stories that promise to bring a touch of sparkle to
your life, with diamond proposals and dazzling weddings,
sparkling brides and gorgeous grooms!

Collect all six books in February 2009,
featuring *Two Little Miracles* by Caroline Anderson.

*Look for the Diamond Brides miniseries
in February 2009!*

HARLEQUIN *Romance.*

This February the Harlequin® Romance series
will feature six Diamond Brides stories featuring
diamond proposals and gorgeous grooms.

Share your dream wedding proposal and you could WIN!

The most romantic entry will win a diamond
necklace and will inspire a proposal in one of
our upcoming Diamond Grooms books in 2010.

In 100 words or less, tell us the most romantic
way that you dream of being proposed to.

For more information, and to enter
the Diamond Brides Proposal contest, please visit
www.DiamondBridesProposal.com

Or mail your entry to us at:

IN THE U.S.: 3010 Walden Ave., P.O. Box 9069, Buffalo, NY 14269-9069
IN CANADA: 225 Duncan Mill Road, Don Mills, ON M3B 3K9

You're invited to join our Tell Harlequin Reader Panel!

By joining our new reader panel you will:

- Receive Harlequin® books—they are FREE and yours to keep with no obligation to purchase anything!
- Participate in fun online surveys
- Exchange opinions and ideas with women just like you
- Have a say in our new book ideas and help us publish the best in women's fiction

In addition, you will have a chance to win great prizes and receive special gifts!
See Web site for details. Some conditions apply.
Space is limited.

To join, visit us at
www.TellHarlequin.com.

HARLEQUIN®

Super Romance®

COMING NEXT MONTH

#1542 THE STORY BETWEEN THEM • Molly O'Keefe
Jennifer Stern has left journalism to focus on life with her son. Then
Ian Greer—son of a former president—picks her to tell the true story of
his family, and it's a scoop she can't resist. But could her attraction to Ian
jeopardize the piece?

#1543 A COWBOY'S REDEMPTION • Jeannie Watt
Home on the Ranch
Kira Jennings just wants access across Jason Ross's land so she can subdivide
her property and sell it off…and save face with her CEO, aka grandfather.
Sure, there's bad blood between Jason and her brother. She didn't realize
exactly *how* bad. Until now.

#1544 THE HERO'S SIN • Darlene Gardner
Return to Indigo Springs
Good thing Sarah Brenneman doesn't judge a book by its cover. Otherwise she'd
believe what the town's gossips say about Michael Donahue. Instead, she's
impressed by his heroics. Still, can she believe what her heart is telling her
about Michael, or could those rumors end their romance before it even begins?

#1545 A KID TO THE RESCUE • Susan Gable
Suddenly a Parent
Shannon Vanderhoff knows that everybody and everything are temporary
gifts. So when she becomes guardian of her six-year-old, traumatized nephew,
how can she give him the help he needs without falling for him? It takes
Greg Hawkins's art therapy class to turn the child around…and it takes a kid
to create this loving family.

#1546 THE THINGS WE DO FOR LOVE • Margot Early
The man Mary Anne Drew loves is marrying someone else. So she buys a love
potion to win him back. Too bad the wrong man drinks it! Graham Corbett has
never shown any interest in Mary Anne before. Could the potion really work?
Or was she looking for love in the wrong place all along?

#1547 WHAT FAMILY MEANS • Geri Krotow
Everlasting Love
Debra and Will Bradley wanted their kids to know that family means
everything. Through hard and joyous times, Debra and Will have never
questioned that. Now Angie, their daughter, is pregnant—and separated.
Award-winning author Geri Krotow tells a memorable story of how marriage
and family define our lives.

HSRCNMBPA0109